Ghosts, Lies, AND Alibis

LAGUNA BAY MIDLIFE WITCH
COZY MYSTERY BOOK 2

Ghosts, Lies, and Alibis

LAGUNA BAY MIDLIFE WITCH COZY MYSTERY BOOK 2

DEANNA DRAKE

Fine Skylark Media

California

Fine Skylark Media
P.O. Box 1505
Lake Forest, California 92630

Ghosts, Lies, and Alibis
Laguna Bay Midlife Witch Cozy Mystery Book 2
Copyright © 2026 by DeAnna Drake
ISBN: 978-1-957691-04-6

Cover Design by Mariah Sinclair

Thank you for supporting indie authors! Your purchase helps keep the magic alive in Laguna Bay and Citrus Grove.

If you enjoy this book and want others to discover Boo, Kheppy, Rebecca, Aneksi, and all the cats who secretly run the universe (at least in our humble opinion), please encourage friends to buy their own copy rather than sharing this file.

Piracy hurts small creators, and your support means the world.

With whiskers, warmth, and gratitude,

DeAnna Drake

Contents

About the Book

Ghosts, Lies, and Alibis

Laguna Bay Midlife Witch Cozy Mystery
Book 2
by DeAnna Drake

—ele—

A body in the milkweed. A talking cat. And a midlife witch in over her head.

Boo Boudreaux thought running the Halloween Boo-tique in the quirky coastal town of Laguna Bay was plenty of excitement for one midlife witch. But when a nosy reporter turns up dead—and her restless spirit refuses to move on—Boo finds herself caught up in long-buried secrets, a fiery tragedy, and a powerful family desperate to keep the past hidden.

With her sassy, magical cat Kheppy at her side and a secret supernatural community watching from the shadows, Boo dives into a paranormal mystery that tests her wit, her heart, and her courage.

Perfect for fans of paranormal cozy mysteries, magical cats, and midlife witch heroines, *Ghosts, Lies, and Alibis* delivers charm, humor, and heart in every page. Grab your favorite brew and settle in—this witch has work to do.

Letter from Boo

Hey there, friend—

Name's Boo Boudreaux. And no, I wasn't born with that name—I picked it for myself when I was seven, after declaring Halloween the best day of the year and deciding I'd never answer to anything else again. Turns out, nobody in Laguna Bay was brave enough to argue with a girl holding a plastic scythe and a sugar high.

These days, I run the Halloween Boo-tique, a little year-round shop filled with spooky delights, vintage décor, and the occasional magical oddity I swear I didn't mean to stock. I share my home (and my headaches) with my younger sister, Delphine, who knows her way around a cauldron better than most, and with Khepeset—who prefers to go by Kheppy—an ancient talking cat who once lounged in Cleopatra's palace and now sleeps on my clean laundry.

I used to read tarot cards. Was pretty good at it, too. But I don't do that anymore. And no, I'd rather not talk about why.

What I will tell you is that Laguna Bay might look like your average coastal town—but that's just the cover. We're a haven for folks with... well, let's call them extraordinary complications. And while I don't consider myself the magical type anymore, Del and I help keep the town's protection spells running smoothly through the Laguna Bay Horticultural Society. It's mostly garden witches and strong tea, but it does the job.

In *Ghosts, Lies, and Alibis*, the past refuses to stay buried. A nosy reporter winds up dead, old secrets rise from the ashes of a long-forgotten fire, and a ghost decides my shop is the perfect place to haunt. Between dodging small-town gossip, pesky politicians, and one very persistent spirit, I'm forced to face a few ghosts of my own—both literal and otherwise.

So pull up a chair, pour yourself a cup of something warm, and settle in.

We've got mysteries to solve, relationships to mend, and—of course—an opinionated cat who's never far away.

Welcome to Laguna Bay.

Warily yours,

Boo Boudreaux

WELCOME TO

LAGUNA
BAY

Chapter 1

Banner Day

MERLE FOSTER GRIPPED THE left side of his campaign banner, while I tugged the cord on the right to lift it over the window of my Halloween Boo-tique specialty shop.

"A little higher on your end, Boo," he called, those burly arms stretched high enough to test the seams of his new western shirt. Judging by the creases still clinging to the fabric, he'd yanked it straight from the package before putting it on.

Typical Merle.

"I know," I said through clenched teeth, though the banner clearly had other ideas. The vinyl slipped from my fingers and dropped onto my head, blinding me with a curtain of my own electric blue hair—the shade I'd chosen on a rebellious whim and kept because, well, it suits me.

Inside my year-round Halloween store, Khepe-set—Kheppy for short—sat perched behind the window, watching our struggle with her knowing feline grin. The gray tabby cat's tawny eyes crinkled just enough to make her amusement obvious. No words necessary.

And thank goodness for that. The last thing I needed was her running commentary while I wrangled with the uncooperative sign. My patience was already whittled to nearly nothing, and another word out of her might have sent me over the edge.

Besides, after a lifetime with that creature, I already knew exactly what she'd say—something she considered helpful, no doubt. Or maybe a suggestion that I wouldn't be in this predicament at all if I had spent more of my time in the Girl Scouts learning to tie proper knots and less time squirreling away boxes of cookies.

Thankfully, the glass was between us, and Merle, who had recently learned about Kheppy's gift of the gab, had the good sense to remain quiet.

"You know, we could've hired someone for this," I muttered, yanking the cord tighter and trying again to form the knot.

Merle shook his head. "It's no worse than when you helped me hang curtains in my first apartment. Remember that?"

"I remember," I said. How could I forget? More than forty years had passed, but it felt like yesterday. We'd been friends since we were children but hadn't started dating yet, though I'd begun to notice something different in the way he looked at me. I'd started looking at him differently too.

That day, he'd shown up at my house, arms full of curtain rods and a sad excuse for drapes, wearing the bewildered expression of a man who was still living with shelves made from concrete blocks and castoff wood.

"I don't have a clue what to do with these. Can you help?" he'd asked in that slow and sweet drawl he'd picked up a few years before from watching old John Wayne movies.

Of course, I'd helped.

The curtains were crooked, the rods barely held, and I think we invented new curse words along the way. When the dust finally settled and the job was done, he'd insisted on taking me to dinner to thank me. That led to a first date, a first kiss, and what I thought might be my first shot at true love.

The relationship hadn't lasted long, though. Life got in the way, but we remained friends, and that's what we'd been ever since. It was what I thought we would always be—until he kissed me a few weeks ago.

Now I'm not sure what we are, which frustrates me more than anything. I'm not the kind of person who likes fuzzy lines. My life already has too many of those.

Through the glass, I saw Khepeset's whiskers twitch. She was holding back.

I pinned her with a glare. "Don't you dare," I mouthed.

Merle, oblivious to our silent standoff, tightened his knot. "There. It's about as straight as it'll get. See? I told you we could do it. We make a good team."

Was he talking about the banner? That hopeful smile suggested something else.

Kheppy smirked. She didn't need words. Her look said it all: *I told you that kiss changed things.*

I ignored her amusement and his sheepish glances. Whatever was happening between Merle and me would have to wait. Today, there was too much to do to get tangled up in feelings.

I stood back from the banner to read the thick black letters on white vinyl. *Vote Merle Foster for Mayor.* It wasn't fancy, but it did the job—and with Merle's candidacy barely a month old, the fact he had a campaign at all was a miracle.

Since the Boo-tique had become his campaign headquarters once the after-Halloween sales were done, and I was serving as his campaign manager, I suppose it was *our* campaign.

I was still getting used to that. It had always been my policy to avoid Laguna Bay's politics, yet here I was, smack dab in the middle of the strangest election season in all of my sixty-four years. It had started simply enough—our incumbent mayor was running unopposed until Merle quietly entered the race to protect our secret supernatural community. When the mayor unexpectedly stepped down, things got weird. Tom Dodge, the town's most aggressively pro-development councilman, jumped into the race, followed by Chef Glen Phan, whose entire campaign seemed to revolve around passing out free samples from his Beachside Café menu.

To give the new candidates a fighting chance, city officials came up with a creative interpretation of key clauses in the town's charter to justify delaying the mayoral election by a few weeks. The extra campaign time had passed quickly while the new ballots were printed. It was hard to believe the fast-tracked special election was already just two days away, and that today's outdoor town hall would be the first and only time the three candidates would appear together. City officials had closed Forest Avenue for the last-minute event, giving it a festive, party-like atmosphere, which definitely wasn't how we typically did things in Laguna Bay.

"Why can't anything be easy around here?" I grumbled as Merle and I lugged our stepladders back into the shop.

"When has anything in this town been easy?" Kheppy said with a lazy stretch. "People here love drama. They flock to it like bees to money."

"Bees to honey," I corrected. For a creature who claimed to have been around for centuries, Kheppy still mangled even the simplest phrases.

"That, too," she said before curling up in the window for another nap.

The Boo-tique's front door flew open, and Sissy, my part-time shop clerk and full-time ray of sunshine, bustled in with a bag of paper cups in one hand and a bottle of something purple in the other.

"We're back," she declared. "Delphine had to park in the public lot, but we made it."

That explained my sister's flaming red cheeks and heaving chest as she trailed behind. She could spend hours picking, pruning, and puttering in our backyard garden, but hoofing it from the public lot two blocks away was apparently more than she could handle.

"Need some help?" I asked after setting down my stepladder.

She placed her grocery bag on the counter by the cash register and tried to catch her breath. "I'm fine. Just a hot flash. It'll pass in a minute."

I handed her a napkin from the stack that came with the box of pastries from the Scandinavian bakery across the street that Merle had brought with him, most of which we'd eaten before tackling the banner.

"Thanks." Del grabbed the napkin and wiped it across her dewy forehead.

I watched Sissy take the bags and purple stuff into the back. "I thought you were getting lemonade," I said.

Sissy had suggested we capitalize on the shop's proximity to the town hall stage by handing out free lemonade to thirsty attendees and encouraging them to vote for Merle. It was a good plan, so I sent her off with Delphine to buy supplies.

"That's what I got," she hollered from the back. "Lavender lemonade!" When she returned, she pulled her long, ginger-blond hair into a ponytail, grabbed her apron from the hook behind the register, and tied it around her waist. "I tried it at the farmers' market last week, and it was delicious. I went with…. Forget it. It doesn't matter." She grabbed a clean rag and went to work on the display of witchy coffee mugs that were already plenty clean.

I didn't have to be psychic to know why she'd abruptly dropped the subject. She'd recently broken up with her boyfriend. I didn't know the young man well, but well enough to know Sissy could do better. When she told me a few days ago he'd taken a job on a cruise ship that would be at sea for the next four months, I pretended to be disappointed for her sake. The breakup, she'd insisted, was mutual. I hoped so. Sissy deserved better than that kid, and considering she was still coming to terms with recent revelations about her and her adopted mother's shape-shifting family history, I'd say the girl had enough to deal with.

"Lavender lemonade, huh?" It sounded more like an air freshener than something you'd sip on an unseasonably warm November afternoon. But what did I know? Besides, I had a fresh six-pack of my favorite imported orange soda in the office fridge. "I've never heard of it, but if you think folks will like it, that's good enough for me."

When Sissy wasn't looking, I glanced at Merle to see if he was as skeptical as I was.

Delphine must have sensed I was about to put her on the spot, too, because she darted toward the back room. "That folding table I hosed down in the alley must be dry by now. I'll go grab it."

"I'll help you," Merle said and hurried after her.

Cowards. Then again, we'd all been walking on eggshells around Sissy since she'd learned about her supernatural history. I'd tried to make things better by telling her—with her mother's permission, of course—that I knew her secret. I'd also admitted that Delphine and I were what some people called witches, that we could sometimes divine the future and cast spells. I didn't tell her Kheppy could talk, though, or that Laguna Bay was full of supernatural people of one type or another who lived among the ordinary humans undetected. Better to let her get comfortable with her own situation before springing that on her.

That's why I busied myself with my own tasks and let the conversation lapse.

When Del and Merle returned, carrying the six-foot-long folding table through the shop, Del looked more like her usual self.

"That milkweed is really taking over back there," she said. "Looks a little parched, though."

"I'll water it when we're done here," I told her as I dumped a bag of *Merle for Mayor* buttons into a basket to hand out with the lemonade.

Delphine clucked her tongue. "Don't wait too long. You'll cause root rot if you water too late in the day."

"It'll be fine," I assured her as Merle muscled the front door open so they could get the table out to the sidewalk.

The glance she shot me said loud and clear: it was not fine. Thankfully, the commotion brewing outside the shop stopped her from pursuing it.

It got my attention too.

Tom Dodge, a short, wiry man decked out in a gray pin-striped suit, was trying to weave around a young woman in a tweed blazer and jeans who was holding a reporter's notepad.

"I understand you were pushing a new development project regarding the Channel Hotel site in a closed City Council session last week. Care to comment?" she demanded.

Councilman Dodge forced a laugh as he smoothed his pencil-thin mustache. "That would be premature, Fiona. But I can tell you I'm always in favor of projects that will improve the lives of Laguna Bay residents. Anything pertaining to that particular site, however, is pure speculation."

Merle took one look at that exchange, lowered his end of the table by the shop's wall, and hustled inside, leaving Delphine to grapple with her end.

The reporter noticed the hasty departure. "Mr. Foster? Would you care to comment on the future of the Channel Hotel site?"

He brushed by me and Sissy like he hadn't heard the question, and disappeared into the back as the young woman followed him inside. She glanced around as she pushed her razor-straight black hair off her shoulder.

"I need to speak with Mr. Foster," she announced.

A door in the back slammed closed. The squeaky hinge told me it had been the bathroom door.

"He may be awhile," I said with a polite smile. I had no idea how long he'd be, but after that hasty retreat, I figured he needed a moment to himself.

The reporter huffed and pulled a business card from her pocket. She handed it to me with a clipped, "Then tell him to call me. It's important."

I flipped the card between my fingers. The front had the Laguna Bay *Gazette*'s information. On the back, scrawled in blue ink, was Fiona Richards and another number.

"May I tell him what it's regarding?" I asked. Frankly, I was curious too.

"I'm working on a story about plans for the Channel Hotel site. I'd like to ask him about the fire that took place there."

"That was at least twenty years ago." I scratched the side of my head as old memories flooded back. The blaze had left a scar on this town, and I wasn't just talking about the abandoned lot with the scorched ruins of an old Victorian building on the north end of town.

"Thirty years this week." Her jaw tightened around the words.

"Really? I didn't realize it had been that long." My eyes were on her card, but my mind was somewhere else, sifting through the ashes of the past. "Such a horrible ordeal."

Her lips curled into a sneer. "It was horrible all right. I know the truth about what happened that night, and soon the rest of Laguna Bay will know it too."

Before I could ask what she meant, she stormed out the door.

Chapter 2

Milkweed

"So, that's Fiona Richards," Delphine mused after the *Laguna Bay Gazette* reporter nearly knocked her over as she stomped out of the Boo-tique.

I glanced up from the business card Fiona had left behind. "You've heard of her?"

"Sure. She's the one who wrote about the City Council accepting pricey gifts from donors. Country club memberships, fancy trips. Everybody in town was talking about it. Don't you remember?"

"You know I don't read the newspaper. It's bad for my blood pressure."

Del smirked. "Speaking of which, did you take your pill this morning?"

"Yes, *Mother*," I said, laying on the sarcasm nice and thick—then winced. Truth was, I didn't always remember, and she knew it. "Sorry, Del. It's just been a weird morning."

Between a rude reporter and Merle acting like he was being chased by a ghost—well, other than Rupert, his longtime spirit companion—I was off-kilter. Not to mention these confusing new feelings between Merle and me.

Delphine patted my back and pushed the droopy strap of my overalls back onto my shoulder like she'd been doing since elementary school. "It's all good. Any idea why Fiona came charging in here?"

"She wanted to talk to Merle about the old Channel Hotel fire."

Delphine accepted another napkin from Sissy, who was passing by on her way out front, lugging a hefty jug of freshly mixed lavender lemonade. "Thanks, dear." Del dabbed at the sweat on her neck. "What's Merle got to do with that?"

"Absolutely nothing," came Merle's booming voice from behind us. "And that's exactly what I'm going to tell that reporter. Where'd she go?"

"She's gone," I said. As if he didn't already know. "Why all the theatrics?"

He snatched his cowboy hat off the counter and slapped it on like a sheriff gearing up for a high-noon showdown. "Figured it was time to head to the stage. Wanted to make sure I looked my best."

Merle had that rugged, easy charm going for him, sure. But if he did more than brush his teeth and run a comb through that still-impressive head of hair, I'd eat my Birkenstocks. Still, if he wanted to pretend his sudden exit had something to do with fashion and not the spitfire reporter gunning for answers, I wasn't about to call him on it.

12

I handed him the business card, which he tucked into his back pocket without even looking at it. I bit back a sigh. Not a great move, politically or otherwise.

"You should still call her," I said. "It won't look good for the campaign if you're ducking the press. It won't help with our other thing, either."

He knew what I meant. The supernatural side of life in Laguna Bay wasn't something we advertised. And we didn't need a nosy reporter poking around in our business and stirring up trouble.

"I will," he said. "Later. Right now, I need to focus on my speech." He looked down at his shirt and frowned. "Did you see Dodge's suit? Nobody said anything about wearing suits. Should I change?"

"Do you have a suit?" I asked, though I already knew the answer.

"No, but Rupert says I could borrow one. Howard wore a nice three-piece to the local business owners' meeting last month."

I frowned. Did he mean Howard Collins from the hardware store? That was the only Howard I knew, but that man was half Merle's size. I debated whether to mention it.

The way Merle tilted his head toward the empty space next to him, and the expression on his face, told me Rupert must have made the same observation. At least Sissy wasn't around to witness this particular moment of ghost whispering. She didn't know about Rupert, and today wasn't the day to explain how Merle saw spirits.

"The reporter was grilling Councilman Dodge about a development project on the edge of town," Delphine said. "Think it's related?"

"How would I know?" Merle grumbled, glancing at his shirt again, then at his watch.

Delphine flinched, realizing she'd touched a nerve. "Oh, look! The gardening girls are here. I should go say hi."

She beelined outside to greet the other members of what we called the Laguna Bay Horticultural Society, but which could more accurately be described as our unofficial garden witch group. Opal Uttari, who liked to think she was the leader of our little flower-power coterie, was already directing Willa, our oldest and wisest member, and Jemma—our newest and, at forty-seven, youngest—to hand out cups of lemonade as fast as Sissy could fill them. It looked like they had it under control, so I focused on Merle.

A hint of green had crept into his usually ruddy complexion, and his hands trembled. I touched his arm and offered what I hoped was a comforting smile.

"You look great, and you don't need to stress about the speech. Everyone in this town knows how much you love Laguna Bay. Certainly more than Councilman *Dodge-the-Issues*."

That nickname wasn't my invention, but I liked it. Almost as much as I liked *Dodge-the-Truth*, which was the other, even less flattering, nickname that was making the rounds.

Merle stared at the floor. "Maybe I'm getting too old for this."

"Oh, please. You've got more energy than anyone I know—well, maybe not Sissy, but she's twenty-one and basically powered by sugar and caffeine. Those werewolf genes probably help, even if they are dormant."

He chuckled at that, which was the goal. "You know," he mused, "I've never seen a werewolf sleep. Rest, maybe. But not sleep."

I grinned. "We should commission a study."

"But, Boo," he said, turning serious again, "I've been out of the game nearly ten years."

"Retirement is hardly out of the game," I said. "Not the way you do it."

After stepping away from his real estate business, Merle had practically become a one-man neighborhood watch, running the police department's Retired and Senior Volunteer Program, and keeping this town safer with his daily patrols. Laguna Bay would be lucky to call him mayor.

"The town needs someone like you," I added and gave his hand a squeeze.

When he squeezed back, I took a deep breath and asked the question I couldn't seem to shake.

"Why do you think that reporter is so interested in you?"

He sucked in a breath, pulled off his hat, and ran his fingers through his hair. "I really don't know, but I'll call her. I just can't think about all that right now."

If he meant to calm me down, he'd missed the mark. *All that*? What exactly was *all that*?

I didn't get a chance to press him. My attention snagged on a familiar, scowling face outside the window—Cornelia Sloane, our resident vampire and the steely-eyed publisher of the Laguna Bay *Gazette*, looking like she'd gotten up on the wrong side of her coffin. Most folks in town called her The Gatekeeper—a nod to her stranglehold on the paper. But in our not-so-public circle, the name meant something more: she kept any supernatural stories from ever getting into print.

Today, keeping secrets clearly wasn't her top priority. Her angular features had twisted into full-blown disapproval, and one glossy red nail—long enough to double as a letter opener—was jabbing far too close to my sister's face for comfort.

"You have no right to sell anything at this event," Cornelia said, her voice as sharp as a knife blade.

"We're not selling anything," I said, cutting in when Sissy opened her mouth and nothing came out. I pointed at the hand-lettered sign Sissy had taped to the table—*free refreshments* written in bright purple bubble letters. "We're giving the lemonade away. If people want to take a campaign button too, that's their prerogative. What's it to you?"

Cornelia's icy blue eyes narrowed on me, and for a split second, I half-expected her to glamour me into compliance. I'd heard she could do it, though I'd never seen proof, and I certainly wasn't eager to find out.

"It is my event," she said, crisp and deliberate, as if each syllable were carved in ice.

Honestly, why couldn't she burst into flames in sunlight like vampires do in the movies? Sadly, the sun only affects the newly turned, and Cornelia was far from new. Ancient, really—though not quite as ancient as Kheppy, it turns out. Still, it would've been nice to be free of her until nightfall.

"Says who?" I demanded.

She inhaled slowly, as if she were trying to remind herself why she shouldn't snap my neck. "Says me. I'm moderating the event, and the *Gazette* is co-sponsoring it."

Well. That would explain the stick up her backside.

"Should I call someone, Ms. Sloane?" came a high-pitched voice from behind her. Zelda Harcourt, Cornelia's assistant, was already clutching her phone with both hands like it might bite her. That mousy little woman with a head of short, dark curls was a normie, but she'd been with Cornelia for so many years, I had to wonder what she knew about the woman's true nature.

"That won't be necessary," Cornelia said, her gaze locked on me. "Will it, Boo?"

I didn't get a chance to answer because someone else chimed in behind me.

"They're right over here, officer! Vending without a permit, right in front of that ugly Halloween shop."

Ooh, ouch.

I turned around, already bracing myself—and there she was: Eleanor Voss, towering over the crowd in five-inch leopard-print stilettos that matched her suit and personality—bold, brash, unapologetic. In one hand she carried a leather notebook stamped with a golden rampant fox, the emblem of the Voss Family Foundation she now controlled.

I was old enough to remember when the Vosses were revered as one of Laguna Bay's oldest supernatural lineages, their magic and money woven into the town's very foundation. When her father lost Eleanor's mother in childbirth, he'd immersed himself in his business and all but severed ties with our community. Since his death, Eleanor had continued that tradition, preferring cocktail receptions with CEOs and civic leaders to the company of her own kind.

Her backup was a uniformed officer who looked barely old enough to drive and deeply uncomfortable.

"Yes, ma'am, I can take it from here," he said with the energy of someone hoping no one made him do anything official. "You can step back."

Eleanor didn't step back. She walked up to Cornelia, leaned in, and whispered something in her ear.

Cornelia didn't react—not even a twitch—but after a beat, she sighed, and her perfectly controlled indignation deflated a little.

"It's handled," she said coolly, not to Zelda, not to the officer, but to me—like a threat disguised as a favor. Her gaze landed on me, daring me to contradict her.

I turned to Delphine and Sissy. "You heard her. Pack it up. We'll move this inside."

There were a few groans from the gardening girls, but the officer looked relieved and quickly trailed off after Cornelia and Eleanor, with Zelda trying to keep up.

Sissy picked up the basket of campaign buttons and raked her fingers through what was left. "Looks like they were popular. We started with a lot more. That's a good sign, right?"

"Absolutely," I said, brushing my palms together. "But we've also got the best candidate on the ballot. That's the only sign we really need. Right, Merle?"

He'd tipped his hat at me. "I'm certainly going to do my best."

When the time came for speeches, Dodge went first—slick and polished, all gleaming veneers and sound-bites about turning Laguna Bay into a world-class blah-blah-blah and a jewel along the Southern California coastline. He used phrases like "economic revitalization," "strategic partnerships," and "heritage rebranding," and I lost count of how many times he mentioned "creative innovation."

Merle's speech was shorter, warmer, and had a lot more heart. He talked about the small-town charm, the close-knit community, and the way neighbors help each other here. He didn't promise to reinvent the wheel. He promised to keep it from spinning out of control.

Chef Glen Phan, bless him, had apparently forgotten he was expected to speak. He rushed in red-faced and winded, tossed out a handful of generic feel-good lines, and then plugged the Beachside Café's lunch specials before giving an energetic wave and leaving the stage.

Once the town hall finished, I headed back to the shop to close up. I sent Sissy home with a hug, a thank-you, and strict instructions to take the leftover lavender lemonade with her.

With the front locked, the protection candle snuffed, and the shop quiet again, Kheppy padded out from the folded blanket she used as a bed behind the counter. Her tail swished once with theatrical annoyance.

"May we *please* go home now? I'm starving."

"You had kitty treats an hour ago."

"That wasn't a meal. That was a snack."

The joys of feline logic.

"We can go after I water the milkweed," I said. "If it dies, Del will never let me live it down."

Kheppy flopped onto her side like a fainting Victorian socialite. "Fine. But if I die of hunger, I will haunt you."

"Aren't you immortal?" I shot back.

She ignored me.

I grabbed the empty lemonade pitcher, filled it with water, and headed out the back door toward the milkweed patch. The sun had already started its descent, casting long shadows through the alley. As I neared the tall leafy stalks with the tiny yellow and orange flowers, I sensed something was different.

Then I saw it.

The jug slipped from my hand and landed with a *thump* on the ground.

A body—partially obscured by the milkweed stalks. Black hair tangled with leaves. A twisted arm. Legs bent at unnatural angles.

It was Fiona Richards, and she wasn't moving.

Chapter 3

Phantom Flickers

Detective Ernie Platt stood beside me in the alley behind the Boo-tique, raking his fingers through his dark, shaggy hair as I explained how I'd found Fiona Richards's dead body. It was a difficult conversation, considering the first time we'd met was a couple of weeks ago, during the unfortunate cauldron incident that canceled this year's Top Haunt window-decorating contest and landed me on the detective's murder suspect list for a while.

At the time, he'd reminded me of a younger, taller Columbo because of his disheveled appearance and khaki trench coat. When he showed up today wearing the same coat and his dark hair still a tangle of unruly curls, I wondered if the resemblance was intentional.

I was about to ask him if he was a fan of the old detective show as we stood over the reporter's body, lying among the milkweed and gravel, when he suddenly glanced up and asked, "Why was she back here?"

"How should I know?" I hugged myself as a cool breeze swept in from the Pacific Ocean, though it was the sight before us—not the setting sun—that sent a deeper chill through me.

"Did you know her?"

"She came into the shop today. She wanted to talk to Merle," I said, and immediately regretted it. I shouldn't have brought Merle into it.

Platt didn't react. "What about?"

"She said she was working on a story about the old Channel Hotel site." I noticed his nose wrinkle with confusion, so I added, "It's a run-down place on the north end of town. It wasn't so much a hotel as a flophouse for artists and starving-student types. Fiona said this week marks thirty years since it burned down."

He perked up. "The victim said that?"

I nodded. "It was a big deal back then, but the place has been abandoned for years."

There had been occasional efforts to rebuild, but the plans always fizzled out. So it sat, hidden behind a chain-link fence, forgotten by most, and deliberately ignored by those of us who remembered what had happened there.

He scribbled in his notes. "Was Merle Foster involved?"

"No."

The detective kept his eyes on his pad, but one eyebrow spiked at my abrupt answer. Had I sounded defensive? "You know," I added quickly, "I saw her talking to Councilman Dodge earlier. She was asking him if he was involved in plans to develop the site. He seemed annoyed by the question."

That, at least, was true.

The detective made another face. "I'm not surprised. Her articles about city hall have been stirring up plenty of trouble lately. Maybe that's what got her killed."

I stared at him. Fiona's death seemed suspicious to me, too, but I was hoping I was wrong. "Do you think she was murdered?"

He pulled a pair of latex gloves from his pocket, slipped them on, and crouched beside the young woman's body. He touched her wrist lightly. "Scratches. Looks like she fought with someone. See that?" He pointed to the jagged stone near her head. "Maybe she tripped and hit that. Or maybe somebody picked it up and hit her with it. We won't know until the coroner takes a look."

His voice was clinical, but there was something else in it too. A hesitation. Maybe even guilt for disclosing so much to a civilian.

He stood again, cleared his throat, and pulled off the gloves as my shop's back door creaked open.

"There you are," Merle said. "Your front door is wide open—" He stopped mid-sentence as he took in the scene. The detective had arrived in the unmarked car parked a few paces away. A white police van rumbled down the alley toward us. Then he saw the body.

Merle stiffened. "Am I interrupting something?"

Detective Platt didn't hesitate. "Not at all, Mr. Foster. Actually, I have some questions for you." He pulled out his notebook again and flipped back a few pages.

Merle chuckled, but confusion flashed across his face. "Sure, Detective. About what?"

Platt's gaze dropped to Fiona.

Merle followed it, his eyes landing on her crumpled form. He moved closer and sucked in a sharp breath when he recognized her. He stumbled backward. "What happened?"

Before Detective Platt could answer, three forensic specialists poured out of the van with speedy precision, armed with clipboards, cameras, and toolboxes. One waded into the milkweed patch to kneel near Fiona's head. Another searched the area around her loafers. Clicks of a camera shutter punctuated the tension.

The color drained from Merle's face. "Is that the reporter?"

Platt stepped forward. "Did you know the victim?"

"Victim?" Merle echoed. "She's a victim?"

The detective gave him a long, inscrutable look, then repeated, "Did you know her, Mr. Foster?"

Merle lifted his hat and ran his hand through his hair. "Hey, what's with the formality? It's just me. Merle."

"Of course, Mr. Foster. If you don't mind, I have a few questions. Ms. Boudreaux said the victim came by the shop before the town hall to speak with you."

"I said she came by," I jumped in, trying to derail the train I'd set in motion. "I didn't say I knew why. When she saw him, she asked if she could speak to him, but he was on his way to the back of the shop. Indisposed."

Platt's eyebrows scrunched down over his nose.

"Visiting the men's room," Merle offered, obviously mortified.

The detective nodded and flipped back a page in his notepad. "Ms. Boudreaux, you said the victim asked about the Channel Hotel fire—the one from thirty years ago?"

"Yeah, I guess I did," I muttered.

I wasn't helping, and I knew it. Platt's jaw tightened, and Merle shot me a bewildered look that made me want to sink into the gravel.

"Maybe we should continue this conversation at the station," the detective said to Merle.

Merle paled. He tried to disguise it with a shrug. "Sure. I'll just make sure Boo's okay, and I'll come right down."

The detective continued to glare. "It would be best if we went together. Do you mind getting in the car?"

Merle tried to smile. It didn't stick. He hooked his thumbs behind his leather belt, but I noticed the sweat stains creeping from under the arms of his brand-new shirt.

"Am I under arrest or something, Detective?"

Platt didn't laugh. He didn't even smile. "Sir, that's not my preference, but I'll leave it up to you."

Funny how some choices really aren't choices at all.

Merle swallowed hard. He reached into his front pocket and pulled out his keyring. He handed it to me without making eye contact.

"Make sure the truck gets back to my place, if you would, doll," he said.

"Of course." My voice cracked. "But that's not necessary. Tell him, Detective. He doesn't have to do that, right?"

"Maybe it's a good idea for you to hold onto those keys for now," Platt replied stoically.

I watched Merle climb into the detective's vehicle. It wasn't a black-and-white cruiser, thank goodness, but it still looked daunting. My heart skipped, stumbled, and crashed somewhere near my knees.

I clenched the keys so tightly they bit into my palm.

When the taillights disappeared down the alley, I went back inside. The shop felt colder, quieter. Like the whole place was holding its breath.

Kheppy sat on my desk, her tail wrapped neatly beside her paws. Her amber eyes narrowed in judgment.

"I think I made a big mistake," I said. My voice echoed in the stillness. "I may have gotten Merle into some trouble."

She tilted her furry head but didn't speak.

I paced.

"I have to get him out of it," I said. "I did this, so I have to undo it."

Kheppy's tail twitched.

The overhead lights flickered. The bulbs dimmed, buzzed, then sputtered. A sharp, unnatural chill rolled through the office like a cold, invisible fog. I wrapped my arms around myself and rubbed my sleeves.

"Great," I muttered. "On top of everything else, I've got wiring problems. Again."

"That's not a wiring problem," Kheppy said.

I spun around. "How do you know?"

"It was Fiona's ghost," she said simply. "She was here."

Chapter 4

Stubborn Spirit

I stared at Kheppy, waiting for her to smirk and chide me for being gullible. Only she was still staring at me, as serious as a heart attack. At my age, that was no laughing matter. "Fiona's ghost? You're sure?" My voice rose an octave. Maybe two.

The cat didn't flinch. "She passed through that wall like a breeze. Trust me, it was not the wiring."

I swallowed hard. The chill hadn't lifted. If anything, it seeped deeper, crawling over me like ice. I rubbed my arms and stepped around the desk, careful not to bump the lamp, which glowed weaker than usual.

Kheppy padded after me. "You should talk to her."

I let out a breath. "What, are you an expert on ghosts now? Is this like that tiger-sized secret you dropped on me a few weeks ago?"

"That was not meant to be a secret," Kheppy replied patiently. "I didn't know about my tiger self until Aneksi taught me to reveal it. Transforming took practice. I wanted to be sure I could control it before telling you. I did not want to risk hurting you."

"You seemed to have plenty of control around the were-wolves," I shot back.

Her whiskers twitched. "I did, didn't I?" she said, sounding quite pleased with herself.

I had to admit, she'd earned it. That had been one impressive display.

"But that has nothing to do with our ghost," she added smoothly, steering us back to the problem. "Fiona may be able to tell you why she's here."

Sometimes that cat was downright brilliant. If Fiona could tell us why she was here, maybe she could also tell us who had killed her. That would save us all—especially Merle—a lot of trouble. There was just one problem.

"I've never talked to a ghost," I said. "I don't even know how."

Merle was my go-to medium, and he'd been hauled off to the police station for questioning—thanks to my big mouth.

"You should try. She may not realize she is dead," Kheppy said. "Merle has mentioned it happens, especially after sudden deaths."

I winced at the reminder of the violence that had occurred just beyond my door. That poor girl. I felt bad for her, even if she had been a royal pain in the neck.

"Perhaps a dowsing pendulum would help," Kheppy added.

I sighed. It had been ages—decades, really—since I'd touched my pendulum. I'd set it aside when I'd put away my tarot deck for good. I used to tell people the magic stopped speaking to me, but that was never the truth.

The truth was, I stopped trusting it.

Worse, I stopped trusting myself—to interpret what it revealed, to act on it with wisdom, to bear the weight of what I saw.

During the recent cauldron fiasco, my sister had prodded me to consult the cards, and they had helped. A bit of that lost trust had been restored, but not all of it.

Still, it seemed like my only option. I opened the desk drawer where I'd last seen my pendulum shoved behind the stapler and a cluster of tangled paper clips. My fingers hovered for a second before curling around the pointed brass pendant.

Its familiar weight settled into my palm as I pulled it out. Cold. Heavy. Full of memories.

Dowsing wasn't sophisticated magic, but it worked—more or less—for yes-or-no questions.

At least it didn't require all the fuss and preparation of a proper séance.

As I looked at it, the pendulum seemed to pulse, and the peridot beads worked into its chain glinted in the light.

"I'll ask her simple questions," I murmured, casting a glance toward the back hallway, where I imagined she might be. "If she's confused, perhaps we can help."

Kheppy nodded solemnly. "Be gentle with her. She may be timid."

I doubted it. That reporter had been brash to the point of arrogant. Certainly not timid.

I pinched the end of the chain, letting the brass weight hover over the desktop.

"Fiona? Are you here?"

The overhead lights flickered—twice. I held my breath, waiting for the pendulum to swing. Back and forth meant yes. A circle meant no. At least, that's how it used to work.

"Do you remember what happened to you?" I asked.

The bob swayed slowly before coming to a stop.

"Do you know who hurt you?"

The bob twitched, then spun slightly in place. No clear answer. Just a sick twisting in my gut.

"Maybe you're right, Khep," I whispered. "Maybe she is timid or confused."

Kheppy didn't reply.

The air shifted again, then Fiona shimmered into view.

Her edges blurred like a flame flickering in fog. Her mouth moved, though no sound emerged, and her eyes locked on mine with such intensity I couldn't look away. She raised a hand, trembling, as if trying to reach for something. Or someone.

"Fiona," I said carefully, "you're not alone. We want to help you. Do you remember what happened?"

Her form shimmered—then vanished.

The lights surged and something popped. I stumbled back, grabbing the edge of the counter.

"She's gone," I gasped.

"No," Kheppy said, jumping onto the desk beside me. "She is still here."

An icy chill hit me. Not just passing around me—but through me.

The sensation sucked the air from me. Cold filled my chest, my belly, my skull. Darkness swallowed the light, then from somewhere far away, I heard Kheppy say my name.

And then—

Fire, roaring and consuming. A hallway choked with smoke. Shadows scrambling.

A scream—a woman's scream.

A hand. Burned. Reaching.

A silver ring. Gleaming. Fingers clutching.

The reek of singed hair. Ash clogging my throat.

Then silence.

When my eyes opened, I was staring at the ceiling with a familiar sensation on my chest.

Kheppy.

Her whiskers tickled my cheek as her face hovered above mine.

"You are not dead," she announced. "Thank the goodness."

I didn't have the energy to correct her. "How long was I out?"

"Two minutes." Her tone was clipped, but there was worry in her eyes. "You stopped moving. Another minute and I would have clawed through a window screen to get help." She jumped off, but kept her eyes on me.

I sat up too fast, and the world wobbled around me. "Two minutes? That's nothing."

"You stopped breathing for thirty seconds," she said. "That is not nothing."

I spit a tuft of fur off my lip. "Great. Now I'm choking on cat hair."

She sniffed. "I was listening for your breath."

My heart pounded, but everything else felt unfortunately familiar. Achy hips. Sore ankles. Honestly, I couldn't remember a day when I didn't roll out of bed and something already hurt. So, no worse than usual.

"I'm okay," I said, rubbing my temples. "I think."

Kheppy didn't appear convinced. "Define okay."

I stood without falling. Progress. I walked around the desk, legs stiff, back tingling like I'd napped on concrete—which, considering the age on that worn carpet, I practically had.

"She passed through me," I said quietly.

Kheppy perked up. "And?"

"She showed me things. Just flashes." I touched my chest, still cold beneath my shirt and overalls. "There was fire. Screaming. And a silver ring."

"Was it the fire she mentioned?"

"I don't think so. The hotel fire happened before she was born. Maybe she was in another fire. Maybe that's why this one hits close to home."

Kheppy tilted her head. "Did you see faces?"

I shook my head. "Mostly shadows."

I looked at the pendulum lying on the desk. Useless.

"She's scared," I said, not knowing exactly how I knew that, but knowing it was true. "She needs help."

"Our help?" Kheppy asked.

I nodded.

"Are you sure you want to get involved? You could tell the police."

If I didn't know better, I would have assumed Delphine had shown up to lecture me. But I did know better, and I knew Kheppy was using her ability to imitate others, especially those she knew well, with uncanny accuracy. I glared down at her. "Don't do that. I'm too tired, and it's too much. But your point is well taken."

Her chin dipped. "Apologies, Boo. I am only concerned about you."

I rubbed her head, and she leaned into me.

"I know you are, and I appreciate it." Probably more than she'd ever realize.

I drifted to the back door and gazed out at the milkweed silhouetted in the moonlight.

"The problem is, I pulled Merle into this mess. And I can't exactly tell that detective—or anyone at the station—about Fiona's ghost. Like it or not, she's our best shot at finding her killer. Maybe our only shot."

There was something else stirring inside me too. I hadn't liked that reporter when she was alive, but death has a way of putting things into perspective. When she passed through me, I'd felt things. Maybe from her past, or maybe something else, but, well, I felt sorry for her.

"Why do you think she's here?" It was a musing sort of question that I didn't really expect Kheppy to answer.

That didn't stop my friend from offering her opinion. "She was working on something. It must have been important to her. Maybe she will not rest until it is finished. Merle says that, doesn't he? That ghosts sometimes linger because of unfinished business?"

I nodded slowly. "Merle has said something to that effect. But what if that story is what got her killed?"

The shop fell silent again. A tense silence, like the walls themselves were listening.

Kheppy nuzzled my hand. "What are you going to do?"

I reached for the pendulum and put it back in the drawer. "What I have to do. I have to figure out who killed her."

"For Merle?" she asked.

"Yes," I said. "But not just for him."

I grabbed my purse and turned off the lights. When I locked the front door behind me, letting the bolt click shut beneath my fingers, I stared through the glass at the hallway behind the counter.

"I have to do it for her too," I added softly to the warm, furry cat cradled in my arm.

Fiona may have been pushy, nosy, and a terrible thorn in my tail, but maybe she was that way because the world had been cruel to her. Maybe she was a brat because no one had ever helped her be better. Maybe she just deserved some compassion.

As I headed down the sidewalk toward my car, I whispered into the darkness, "We're going to figure this out, Fiona. I promise."

The wind rustled through the trees as if in answer.

And I hoped, wherever Fiona was, she'd heard me.

Chapter 5

Leftover Gumbo

OUR SCREEN DOOR CLATTERED shut behind me with a sharp clang.

"Easy," Kheppy murmured, padding along beside me. "Your aggravation's showing."

She wasn't wrong. My emotions were getting the better of me. I ran a hand over my face and drew in a long, steadying breath.

The moment I stepped into the warm glow of our front room, the tightness in my chest eased. Delphine had lit a few candles—on the coffee table and beside the television cabinet—and Loreena McKennitt's soothing melodies floated from the stereo, filling the space with an enchanting sense of calm.

"Before you get too comfortable, you've got mail," Delphine called from the kitchen. A neat stack of envelopes waited on the table by the door. Bills, grocery circulars, the usual. One piece caught my eye. A fancy envelope, its edges trimmed in delicate flowers. A New Orleans postmark peeked out from the corner. My chest tightened. Not now. I slid the letter aside for later. I couldn't deal with that tonight.

After dropping my purse onto the nearest armchair, atop the crocheted afghan dusted with cat hair, I focused on letting the tension melt away.

A deep, calming breath hinted at something savory underway in the kitchen. I knew better than to get my hopes up, though. Delphine had fooled me plenty of times since she'd gone vegan. A delicious smell didn't always equal a delicious meal. I'd learned that the hard way.

A sudden pang of worry struck. "Wait, I thought we canceled Sunday dinner this week. Did I miss it?"

Family dinner had been our Sunday night tradition since my granddaughter, Luna, had moved to Citrus Grove, a charming town about twenty miles away. It was something I always looked forward to, but with my campaign duties this weekend and Luna working hard on her new bakery, we'd decided to skip a week. At least I thought we had.

"No, no," Delphine said, peeking out from the kitchen doorway. Her silver hair was braided and pinned into a halo around her head, and a sheen of sweat clung to her temples. Either she'd been hovering over the stove too long, or her hot flashes were back. "Luna sends her love. I'm just experimenting with a new recipe. But where have you been? Were you and Merle working late on his campaign?"

I ignored her teasing smirk and joined her at the stove, where she was stirring lumps of something floating in a stockpot.

"I don't even know where to begin," I said. It was the truth. A dead body? Merle practically arrested? The ghost? That ache tunneling behind my eyes told me I needed an aspirin. Or food. Probably both.

Delphine either didn't pick up on the grump in my grumpy response or was pretending she hadn't because she glanced at me, beaming. "You're just in time to try the seitan."

"The say-what?" I asked, but I was pretty sure I didn't want to know the answer. I moved toward the fridge to find something more recognizable.

"It's wheat gluten," she said, as if I should know what that meant.

I didn't.

"It's a wonderful source of protein," she continued. "I've already made a batch." She nodded toward a covered plate on the counter. "Help yourself. It tastes like chicken."

I gave her a look as I grabbed the container of leftover chicken and sausage gumbo. Since she'd gone vegan, I'd learned to stash away any good stuff when I had the chance.

"If you're trying to make something that tastes like chicken," I said, prying off the gumbo's lid, "why don't you just use chicken?"

"Cholesterol," she said as she crumbled something that looked like beige gravel into the pot. "Plant-based diets have many health benefits."

"So I've heard." I cut a slice of soda bread still warm from the oven.

I'd remembered to take my blood pressure pill that morning, so as far as I was concerned, I was winning on the health front.

Kheppy leaped onto the counter and glared at me. "Are you going to tell her what happened at the shop?"

"Can I heat up my dinner first?" I shoved my bowl of gumbo into the microwave and set it for a couple of minutes.

"Tell me what?" Delphine asked. "What happened at the shop?"

"A lot." I sealed up the remaining gumbo and returned it to the fridge, pushing the container all the way to the back so my sister wouldn't toss it out during one of her cleaning fits.

Delphine continued to stir her lumpy brew. "I'm listening."

"Well, I found that reporter's body in the alley behind the shop when I went to water the milkweed." It hadn't occurred to me until that moment that I never would have seen Fiona if it weren't for my sister and that thirsty milkweed.

I was pulling a soup spoon out of the drawer when an abrupt clatter made me jump. Delphine had dropped the metal spatula she was using to stir her fake food.

She spun around, ignoring the utensil lying in a brown puddle on the linoleum. "You found what?"

I laid out the whole horrible ordeal.

Delphine gasped. "Oh, my stars. Was she—?"

"Dead as disco," I said, pulling my dinner from the microwave. It smelled even better when it was piping hot, but the image of that poor woman in the alley soured my stomach. I set the bowl on the counter, next to my abandoned slice of bread.

Delphine rescued the spatula and tossed it in the sink before sinking herself into one of our mismatched kitchen chairs, fanning her face. "That must have been an awkward conversation with the detective. Two bodies have now shown up at your shop."

"No," I said, plopping down in the seat across from her. "Fiona wasn't in my shop. She was outside. Totally different."

I knew it wasn't different, and I'd seen the look on Detective Platt's face. He might be new to Laguna Bay, but he wasn't new to dead bodies or suspicious circumstances.

Delphine gave me a long look that said she wasn't buying it, either.

"You need to keep your nose out of this one," she said. "We got lucky the first time. Platt's only been with Laguna Bay PD a month. He hasn't had time to notice how strange things can be around here. If he digs around in the wrong places, he might find something we don't want him to find."

The lid she'd put on her pot rattled. She jumped from her seat and grabbed a fresh wooden spoon to give the concoction a stir before it boiled over.

"We don't need more trouble," she added, setting the lid on the pot with enough space for steam to escape.

"I know," I said, softening. "But he took Merle in for questioning. I think he's a suspect."

Delphine turned. "What? Why?"

I looked at Kheppy, who was curled on a stool, her tail tucked neatly as she stared at me like a judgmental little loaf.

"I might have mentioned that Fiona came to the shop to see Merle."

Delphine narrowed her eyes. "That doesn't sound so bad."

"And I might have given the impression that Merle was avoiding her."

"Oh," Delphine said. Just one word, but its weight clunked down between us like an anvil. Even Kheppy winced.

I pushed a chunk of my electric blue hair back behind my ears. "I didn't mean for it to sound bad, but I think it did. The detective was staring at me like I was hiding something, and it just came out."

Delphine moved closer and put her hand on my shoulder. She squeezed it gently. "Don't beat yourself up. I'm sure it will be fine. Merle didn't kill that woman."

I nodded, but the guilt remained.

"When are you going to tell her about the ghost?" Kheppy asked, impatience in her voice.

Delphine's hand froze on my arm. "There's a ghost?"

I took another deep breath. "Yeah, there's a ghost."

Delphine sat and leaned forward. "Why is there a ghost in your shop?"

"Beats me. She just showed up," I said.

"It's Fiona's ghost," Kheppy added.

Delphine sat back. "What does she want?"

"We don't know," I said. "I tried to talk to her. I even used the pendulum. Right, Kheppy?"

The cat gave a single, solemn nod. "She did, but it didn't work."

"You made her leave, though. Right?" Delphine pressed.

I shook my head.

"Don't tell me you left her there." Delphine glared at me.

I threw up my hands. "What was I supposed to do? Bring her home with me?"

Delphine's expression said yes. That was exactly what I should have done.

"I don't even know how to do that," I admitted. "You know I don't do ghosts. That's Merle's department."

I glanced at my phone for the tenth time that hour. Still nothing from him. No texts. No calls.

Three hours of questioning was a long time for someone who hadn't done anything wrong.

I jammed my hand into the front pocket of my overalls and found the ring of keys Merle had given me. I'd forgotten all about them. His truck—his precious, meticulously polished truck—was parked somewhere along Forest Avenue, waiting.

I hadn't done much right today, but I could at least do that.

I pushed away from the table and got to my feet.

"Where are you going?" Delphine asked, startled.

"I have to get Merle's truck to his place," I said, grabbing my *Witchy Vibes* hoodie to fight off the evening chill.

"You're going now?" she barked.

"It's the least I can do."

Delphine got up, turned off the stove, and stepped in front of me, blocking my path to the door. "If you're going, I'm going with you."

Her voice had gone soft. Sisterly. We'd grown up fighting like cats and dogs, but lately, we'd become more like bookends—opposite, but both devoted to holding things together. Even if she was technically my little sister, she was the steady one now.

"I'm okay," I said. "Really. I know you're busy. I can do this."

Delphine smiled, but there was a shadow of worry in her eyes. "The seitan can wait, and I've already tended to the laurel patch in the garden. We'll have fresh leaves for next week's horticultural society meeting."

"You've been busy," I said, grateful for the change in subject—and for the fact we now had the key ingredient for our New Moon protection spell. If that charm ever failed, we'd light up like a beacon for every supernatural predator on the West Coast. The haven we'd built could unravel in a heartbeat. "But you really don't have to."

She tilted her head, giving me that look—half sisterly patience, half stubborn dare. "I'm coming. We'll handle this together. Besides, you'll need another driver."

She wasn't wrong. If I drove Merle's truck back to his place, I wasn't about to hoof it back home. A few miles in the dark with only my thoughts for company? Hard pass. Having Delphine follow me in my car was the smarter move.

Kheppy leaped up beside me as I opened the door. "If you don't mind, I prefer to stay here."

"I don't mind at all," I said, holding the door for Delphine. "Somebody needs to keep an eye on the place."

The smug glint in her eye said, *of course the job should fall to me*, before she padded over to her favorite armchair.

Outside, the night air nipped at my cheeks, sharp and brisk. The scent of salt drifted in from the ocean, mingling with the sweet perfume of night-blooming jasmine that climbed along the side of our house. Somewhere nearby, a wind chime whispered in the breeze.

I tightened my grip on Merle's keys. This wouldn't undo the damage I'd done, but it was something. Tonight, it would have to be enough.

Chapter 6

The Beast

My Karmann Ghia growled louder than usual as we barreled down the canyon road toward the Boo-tique. Wind knifed through the stuck driver's-side window as Delphine wrestled with the heat dial, trying to summon some warmth against the night's bracing chill.

With a sigh, she gave up on the heater and folded her arms, one hand gripping the seatbelt like it was a lifeline. Not that I could blame her. I was in a hurry, and I wasn't about to let a speed limit slow me down.

"You should have brought something to eat," she said, half-yelling over the wind's howl. "You didn't finish your dinner, and you get hangry when you're stressed."

"I'm not hangry," I muttered, glaring at the center line. "And I'm not stressed."

"Mmm-hmm," she said, in that sisterly tone that sounded suspiciously doubtful. "You're not upset that Detective Platt carted off Merle?"

"He wasn't carted off," I snapped. "He walked. Voluntarily. I think."

She gave me a sideways glance, then adjusted the crocheted scarf she'd tied around her neck. A soft lavender hue that flattered her complexion.

I focused on the road. The fog was clinging low to the pavement and turning the streetlights into halos of shimmering mist.

"You two looked cozy putting up that banner today," she said eventually, like it was an afterthought instead of a topic she'd been dying to bring up since I got home.

"Cozy? We bickered over everything. It didn't feel cozy."

She shrugged. "I know you better than that. Both of you. It was cozy. So, how are things going between you since, well, you know."

Since he kissed me. Strange how something so simple could still stir up feelings I hadn't felt in years. That silly grin on Delphine's face told me she was feeling it too.

I sighed. "We're still figuring it out. Or I am. I thought I was too old for this." Certainly too old to feel all goofy and squishy inside.

"Well, for what it's worth, I think you two make a great couple. You're good for each other."

I wasn't sure how to respond. It had been a long time since I'd thought of myself as part of a couple. It had been Delphine, Kheppy, and me for so long. After Lila's father and everything that had happened when he whisked me off to New Orleans for that whirlwind year, I'd sworn off that kind of partnership for good. That chapter had closed when I'd returned to Laguna Bay, and the ache had faded, but the promise I'd made to myself still stood, clear as ever:

Never allow anyone to get close enough to do that kind of damage again.

As we turned off Forest Avenue, I spotted Merle's truck parked in the lot next to Howard's hardware store. The place looked empty, so I pulled in next to the vehicle and killed the engine.

"All yours," I said as I swung open the door and stepped out. "Treat her well. You know how finicky she can be."

"Are you talking to me or the car?" Del winked. "Just kidding. I'll be gentle. But are you sure you can drive Merle's beast?"

Beast was an appropriate name for that enormous thing. I slapped the side of the giant wheel well. "Sure. How hard can it be?"

Del gave me a look like I might want to reconsider, but before I could assure her I'd be fine, the hardware store's back door creaked open.

Howard Collins stepped out, wiping his hands on a rag that looked like it had seen better days. He wore his usual work apron over a tired flannel shirt and jeans, and I could practically smell the mix of sawdust and linseed oil that always clung to him.

"Thought that was you two," he called. "I saw you on the security camera. Heard about what happened at your shop today, Boo. Such a shame."

"It wasn't at the shop," I corrected. "It was in the alley."

Del chimed in cheerfully. "Boo's a little sensitive about it."

I shot her a look. She smiled innocently.

Howard nodded. "Understandable."

But he wasn't done. There was something else on his mind, and it only took him a moment to get to it. "Since you're here grabbing Merle's truck, the rumors about him being arrested must be true."

His gaze lingered on me, and a chill crept through me. He was one of Merle's closest friends, and I'd never been sure just how strong his psychic abilities really were. As the longtime elder representing mediums and psychics on our supernatural council, though, I had to believe he wouldn't be in that position without the power to back it up.

I scrambled my thoughts with nonsense just in case. My grocery list. The lyrics to that old earworm song about tainted love. Kheppy flicking kitty litter out of her box and scolding me about bathroom privacy when I'd walked in on her that morning. Anything to cloud my mind.

He chuckled softly, which told me he knew exactly what I was doing.

"He hasn't been arrested," I said, lifting my chin. "He's being questioned. Detective Platt doesn't know what's what yet. He's still new."

I didn't mention I'd inadvertently nudged the whole thing along, but the guilt still gnawed at me.

"That reporter was trying to interview Merle about a story she was working on when she died," I added.

I was trying to change the subject, but I was making myself feel worse. Saying the words aloud made my stomach churn.

Howard rubbed his chin. "Is that so?"

"Before she asked about Merle, I overheard her talking to Councilman Tom Dodge. Something about a new development he's trying to push through at the old Channel Hotel fire site. Have you heard anything about that?"

He shook his head slowly, as if weighing his words—or deciding how much to reveal.

The fire had that effect. Just the mention of it was enough to silence people, a tragedy so haunting that those who remembered it wished they could forget.

"Do you think there's a chance Merle could be involved?" I pressed.

Howard scratched his head. "He hasn't mentioned anything."

Okay. Vague.

"He had his real estate business, though. I remember people accusing the woman who owned the place of setting the fire for the insurance money. Do you think she might have tried to sell it first? Maybe she contacted Merle."

Howard gave me a long, hard look. "No, Boo. If she had, I'm sure he would have said so. That fire was a big deal."

It was. I could still remember how the smoke had filled the sky, the sirens, the way the whole town fell quiet for days afterward. People were so frightened that smoldering embers might spark a wildfire that could tear through the canyon.

"If Merle knew anything, he would have said something," Howard said. "He's a good egg."

I knew that. I did. And I hated that a shadow of doubt had even crossed my mind. That wasn't who I wanted to be. Merle had always stood up for me, even when I didn't ask for it. I just couldn't get past the idea that he was hiding something.

"Thanks, Howard," I said.

He nodded. "Let me know if there's anything I can do to help."

He turned back inside. I stood there a moment, the air heavy with salt, mist, and old memories. My fingers curled around the edge of Merle's truck door.

Del had stayed quiet while Howard and I talked, but now she revved the Ghia's engine to get my attention. When she caught my eye, she waved and mouthed, "I'll see you at home."

"Wait!" I jumped behind her to keep her from pulling away.

The car jerked to a stop, and I jogged up to the broken driver's side window.

"Hey," I said, leaning down. "I didn't have any luck talking to Fiona's ghost, but do you want to come by and see if she'll talk to you? Maybe you'll have better luck."

She grinned so wide, it brought out the dimple in her left cheek. "I thought you'd never ask."

"Great," I said and tapped the hood on my way back to the truck. "I'll meet you there."

As Del shifted into gear and pulled out of the lot, I stood in place a beat longer. Merle. The fire. Fiona's ghost. They were pieces of a puzzle, and I could feel them coming together. Somewhere in the middle of it all was the truth. I just hoped I'd find it before Merle paid the price for my careless words.

Chapter 7

F for Fiasco

IF LIFE HAS TAUGHT me anything, it's that the moment you utter the words "This shouldn't take long," you've pretty much guaranteed it will.

Somehow, I still made that rookie mistake just after Delphine and I parked in front of the Boo-tique. We found a pair of spaces easily enough, which I took as a good omen, even if it was the middle of the night and most of the town was asleep.

My plan was simple: slip inside the shop and let Delphine handle the ghost-hunting. Fiona's spirit would appear, or she wouldn't. Either way, I figured we'd be back home in time for the late-night shows, a steaming mug of chamomile tea, and a thick slice of Del's banana bread slathered with her homemade pumpkin butter.

That plan flew out the window the second I opened the door and discovered pure, unfiltered chaos.

"Oh no," Del breathed as she gazed over my shoulder.

My heart dropped straight into my Birkenstocks.

The shelves looked like someone had taken a baseball bat to them. Petunia, my mannequin witch, was face-down in the window display, her cape twisted like she'd been caught in a tornado. A half-dozen plastic jack-o'-lanterns were strewn across the floor, along with the whole display of cinnamon-scented broomsticks. The mini plastic cauldrons had been hurled against the wall, scattering them around the shop like big, black marbles.

But the worst of it—the absolute worst—were two jugs of lavender lemonade Sissy had left behind.

Someone had knocked them over, and the impact popped the caps, flooding the two back aisles with purple stuff. The paper cups and napkins had collapsed into a soggy, lilac-colored mush. Sissy's carefully lettered *free refreshments* sign had been impaled on the tip of a ceramic witch's hat like a defeated battle flag.

"Okay," I said slowly, trying to keep my cool. "This place did not look like this when Kheppy and I left."

Del turned in a slow circle, taking in the chaos. "Oh, Boo."

I stooped to pick up the shattered remains of a ceramic tombstone paperweight—the one that used to say R.I.P. Stress. The irony wasn't lost on me.

"It doesn't look like anything was taken," Del said, frowning. "But who would do this?"

I gave her a look. She had to know.

Her brows lifted. "Do you really think it was Fiona's ghost?"

I didn't want to admit it, but that woman had a mean streak when she was alive. Was it really such a stretch to think that attitude could have followed her to the other side?

"Who else could it be?" I muttered, tossing the tombstone's ceramic shards into the trash. "But the real question is, is she still here?"

Del took a deep breath and glanced around again. I did the same.

"How much did she materialize when you saw her before?" Del asked.

"Not much. I saw something like a shimmer in the air, and then a little of her face. That was it. It only lasted a few seconds."

Del nodded like it meant something. I hoped it did, because I was still clueless.

"Fiona," Del called softly as she wandered down the costume aisle. "Are you here?"

Still nothing.

My sister walked gingerly around the shop, whispering Fiona's name. If I didn't know better, I'd think she was trying to lure a skittish stray cat, not a stubborn ghost.

"Do you really think that's going to work?" I asked.

The frown my sister shot in my direction told me my commentary wasn't helpful or wanted.

"Fine," I muttered and headed to the back to grab a stack of cleaning towels and threw them down on the puddle of lemonade. While Del did her ghost-hunting bit, someone had to clean up.

"She's not here," Del said after I'd mopped up most of the liquid and was working on getting the cinnamon brooms back into their display. "Are you sure what you saw was a ghost? Maybe it was something else."

I propped up the last broom and slapped my hands together to brush away the cinnamon dust. "What else looks like a ghost?"

"You don't have to be so sarcastic," Del snapped. "I'm just trying to help."

"I know. I'm sorry. It's just frustrating. I didn't just see her, I felt her."

The memory hit me again in flashes: the fire, the scorched hand, the glint of that ring. A fresh shiver ran down my spine.

"Kheppy saw her too," I added. "But that still doesn't explain this." I gestured at the chaos around us. "What's the point of smashing plastic pumpkins and toppling poor Petunia?"

My shoulders tensed as I fought the rising urge to scream.

Del shook her head, obviously struggling for an answer as much as I was. "Maybe there's another explanation. Could it have been teenagers?"

"Teenagers would have messed with the masks and the makeup." We could both see those areas were mostly untouched.

"What about the werewolves?" Del suggested. "They can get pretty rowdy."

It wasn't the werewolves. Their claws would have gouged the floorboards, and no amount of lemon, sage, or eucalyptus from the shop candle could disguise their canine musk. I straightened a toppled display of Dead Tired eye masks and tried to ignore the knot tightening in my chest.

"Do you want to know what I think?" Del asked, folding her arms over the fleece cardigan she'd pulled over her T-shirt and jeans. "I think we need the girls. At least Willa. She's dealt with spirits before. We could do a proper séance."

I made a sound that was half snort and half laugh. "You mean out back with the milkweed? The neighbors would love that. Besides, Willa hasn't done a séance in years. She probably wouldn't even want to do it."

Del shrugged. "She might. If you asked her."

"No," I said, maybe too quickly. "I can handle this."

Del hesitated, then nodded. "All right. It was just a suggestion."

Of course. My sister was always trying to help.

She meant well, and I knew that, but I couldn't take her help this time. I couldn't take anybody's help, because I didn't want to drag anyone else into this mess. This was my fault. I'd let things get out of control. Fiona's ghost was in my shop and Merle was in the middle of all this trouble because of me. Somehow, I needed to fix this before it got any worse.

Del wandered toward the front window while I tucked the surviving greeting cards back into their stand. "Hey, Boo?"

"Yeah?"

"You didn't see anyone use this door since we got here, right?"

"Of course not."

"You're sure?"

I dropped the last card into a slot and turned around, my stomach twisting. "Why?"

She was staring at the door's glass panel. It had fogged over in one particular spot, even though the temperature hadn't changed. As I stared at it, trying to puzzle out what could have caused it, something invisible—like a ghostly finger—dragged through the condensation.

It wrote the letter F.

Del's hand gripped the counter. I didn't move. Didn't breathe.

"F for Fiona?" she whispered.

It wasn't the only F-word that sprang to mind. Fiasco topped my list.

The ghost kept writing.

i

Then...

r

And finally...

e

Fire.

The word sat there, staring at us like a warning straight from the other side.

I swallowed hard. "I'd say that confirms that Fiona is still here."

Del blanched. "Do you think she means the Channel Hotel fire?"

"Maybe," I whispered. "Or maybe she's talking about a fire that hasn't happened yet."

We stood in eerie silence, gaping at the foggy scrawl as the chill in the shop deepened around us. I wrapped my arms around myself, but it didn't help. The cold had seeped beneath my skin.

My phone buzzed in my pocket. I jumped, then fumbled to get it out.

Merle.

I answered. "Hey."

"Boo," he said, his voice low and hoarse, like he was tired and talked out. "I just got home. Where's my truck?"

I looked out at where I'd parked it beneath the hazy streetlight.

"I've got it," I said. "I'll be right there."

"Okay." A pause. "Thanks."

The line clicked off.

I turned to Del, who was still staring at the window.

"I have to get the truck back to Merle."

Del's lips pressed into a thin line. "You're sure you don't want his help with this?"

"I'm sure," I said. "This isn't his problem."

She nodded—maybe not believing me, but knowing better than to argue. For a moment, she stared at the window, then glanced at the ceiling. "Fiona? Is there anything else you want to tell us?"

We waited for a full minute, but nothing happened. Slowly, the fog on the glass faded, along with that fateful word.

"I guess that's all she has to say tonight," I said.

Del nodded, but her thoughts seemed elsewhere.

"Do you want to stick around?" I asked. "I can leave the keys."

That snapped her out of it. "Are you kidding? I'm not staying here alone. There's a ghost in here!"

I suppose I couldn't blame her.

"I'll meet you at home, then?" I started to leave but paused. "Fiona, if you're here, could you please leave the merchandise alone? Whatever you need, we'll do our best to help. Just please, don't wreck anything."

I looked at Del. "Think that'll work?"

She shrugged. "Doesn't hurt to try. Should I follow you to Merle's place?"

I knew she was thinking I'd need a ride home. But I was thinking about the conversation I needed to have with Merle, and that would be easier without an audience.

"You go on home," I said. "I'll call if I need you."

I didn't add *when*—no sense tempting fate.

Chapter 8

Person of Interest

MERLE WAS SITTING ON a weathered Adirondack chair on his wraparound porch, smoking a cigar, when I turned onto his street. The house really was something, perched high above the town, overlooking a cascade of cottage rooftops and the ribbon of Coast Highway winding along the shore. On a clear day, you could see Catalina Island on the horizon.

On a clear night like tonight, that horizon all but disappeared. I couldn't tell where the stars in the sky ended and their reflection in the Pacific began. Somewhere below, waves crashed against the shore, slow and steady, like the heartbeat of the town.

When I rolled up to his driveway, a small hatchback pulled away from the curb. As the car passed under a streetlight, I caught the driver's profile—short brunette curls, cat-eye glasses, and that perpetual pout. But what was Zelda Harcourt doing here?

By the time I pulled the truck up to the garage beneath the overgrown magnolia tree, its white blossoms rustling in the breeze, Merle was already stubbing out his cigar and getting to his feet.

The porch light cast a soft golden glow around him, but it couldn't hide the slump in his shoulders or the tired look etched across his face.

It broke my heart to see him so utterly worn out—so different from his usual hearty, confident self, all steel spine and John Wayne swagger. As rough as my night had been, wrestling with a renegade ghost and my sister's questions, I could only guess how much worse it had been for Merle. To think, one minute you're a trusted community figure, the friendly face of the police volunteer unit and mayoral candidate, and the next you're being grilled like a common criminal. That would knock the wind out of anybody.

I reminded myself to tread carefully as I set the emergency brake and eased out of the truck.

He gave me and the vehicle a curious once-over as he approached. "You sounded upset on the phone. If I caught you at a bad time, the truck could've waited."

"It wasn't that," I said, brushing a few stubborn blue strands away from my face. "Was that Zelda Harcourt I saw leaving?"

His mouth hardened into a grimace. "Yeah. Cornelia sent her. She said they wanted to be sure I was available for an interview tomorrow to discuss an editorial endorsement. She's doing a last round of interviews with all the candidates before she makes a decision."

I squinted toward the road. "The day before the election? Isn't it a little late?"

He shrugged, stuffing his hands into the pockets of his jeans. "Probably. I think I know which way the paper—or at least Cornelia—is leaning, but I said I'd be there."

By the sound of it, he didn't seem to think that endorsement was going to go his way. I wanted to reassure him, but I was still stuck on Zelda's late-night visit.

"Couldn't she have called?" I asked.

His head tilted to the side. "Why? Are you jealous?"

I laughed, or tried to. It sounded more like a cat with a hairball, but I still did my best to shake off the implication. "It's just unusual. Don't you think? Especially after..."

I didn't bother stating the obvious. He'd already spent most of the night at the police station, answering questions about the tragedy behind my shop. No sense dragging it out.

He seemed to catch my drift. "I suppose that had something to do with it too," he said with a sigh. "You know how that woman can be."

The way he said *that woman* told me everything. We both knew Cornelia wasn't just a woman. Like most vampires I'd met, she was cool, calculating, and may as well have been carved from granite. As the long-time publisher of the *Gazette*, she'd built a legacy on self-interest and had a knack for delegating the dirtiest work to her minions. Ever since she'd promoted Zelda from receptionist to personal assistant a few years back, that particular minion had become her favorite attack dog.

Even so, the timing felt off.

"Something happened, didn't it?" His eyes narrowed with concern.

"You could say that."

He shoved his hands into his pockets and rocked back on his heels. "Are you going to tell me what it was?"

I could practically see the gears spinning in his head, imagining every worst-case scenario. I didn't know how to ease into it, so I didn't. "Fiona's ghost is haunting my shop."

He frowned. The worry wheels spun faster, trying to make sense of that sentence. "Fiona's ghost?" he asked carefully.

"Yeah. Poltergeist is probably a more accurate description. She really did a number on the place."

"You're sure it's her?"

"Definitely sure," I said. "Kheppy and Del saw her too."

Well, Kheppy had seen her. Del had seen the aftermath and the message in the foggy glass, but it didn't seem worth quibbling over.

Merle lifted his cowboy hat and rubbed his silver-streaked hair. "What does she want?"

"Good question." I kicked a pebble off the drive. "Want to come down and ask her? You're the ghost whisperer."

I expected a chuckle, or maybe an eye roll. Instead, he winced. "You want me to go down there now?" His nose wrinkled, a subtle hint he really didn't want to. "I just got back from the police station, and it's been such a long day."

"You're right. It can wait." I gave him a small smile.

He nodded gratefully.

"What happened at the station, anyway?" I asked. "They let you go. Does that mean you aren't a suspect?"

"Not a suspect," he confirmed. "Not officially. The term they used was person of interest."

"Well, they're not wrong. I think you're interesting."

That earned me a smile.

He looked past me, toward the road. "Del didn't follow you?"

"Nope."

He gestured at the house. "Want to come inside? I've got lemonade. The real stuff. Not whatever that flowery stuff was that Sissy was handing out."

He knew me so well.

"As tempting as that sounds, I should be getting home. It's a work night."

The spark behind his eyes dimmed. I could see his disappointment, but I wasn't ready for lemonade, or whatever else he was suggesting.

"Sure," he said. "Should I drive, or do you want to do the honors?"

I was already halfway to the passenger side. "It's all yours, cowboy. I got her here, but just barely. Driving this thing is like driving a two-story building. I don't know how you do it."

"It's like most things," he said, climbing into the cab. "You get used to it."

As we motored down the hill, the silence between us stretched. We were halfway to my place when I finally mustered the nerve to break it.

"So," I said, keeping my voice light, "what did you and Detective Platt talk about?"

Even in the moonlight, I could see his muscles twitching just beneath the surface.

Wrong topic, Boo.

"The usual," he said flatly. "Where I was, what I knew about the victim, whether I knew of any enemies."

"Do you?"

He glanced at me, then back at the road. "No. I told you, Boo. I don't know what happened to that woman, and I didn't have anything to do with it. It sounds like you don't believe me."

"I believe you," I said, and I meant it. Mostly. "It just felt like there was something more. Like maybe you were protecting somebody."

His grip tightened on the steering wheel as he turned onto my lane. The road was dark because the streetlight was out, but I could see my little Ghia in the driveway.

He eased in behind it and killed the engine.

"Do you want to come in?" I asked. "Del made banana bread."

He shook his head. "It's late. And a work night."

Ouch. Using my own excuses against me. I opened the door and stepped out, hesitating slightly before approaching his window.

He rolled it down and leaned out. "Boo, I'm telling you the truth. I had nothing to do with what happened to Fiona Richards, and I'm not protecting anyone. I wish you'd believe me."

"I do," I said. But the words felt weaker than they should have.

He nodded once, slow and resigned, then rolled off my driveway and back toward the road.

I stood there, watching his taillights fade into the mist. He didn't believe me. And the worst part was, I wasn't sure I believed myself.

Chapter 9

The Damage

THE CHIME ABOVE THE Boo-tique's front door let out a half-hearted wheeze as I shoved it open. I didn't wait for the full jingle. I was too busy stepping over the toppled display of felt witch hats, ducking under a swaying shelf of plastic black cats, and trying not to twist an ankle on a shattered ceramic jack-o-lantern. "Fiona," I said, dragging out the name with barely controlled frustration. "Why are you destroying my shop?"

No reply. Not even a whisper or a shimmer of ghostly mist. Just silence, and the faint smell of lemon, eucalyptus, and sage as I lit the shop's protection candle.

I rubbed my temple. The pounding behind my eyes had started around dawn, after Kheppy demanded to be let out of the room. She'd tolerated exactly one hour of my tossing and turning before hopping off the bed with a low-throated grumble that needed no translation. *You're annoying. I will find other accommodations.*

I'd considered reminding her of all the cat fur in the face I'd endured over the years from her nocturnal acrobatics, but I didn't have the energy to argue. Instead, I'd crawled out of bed at first light, brewed the strongest black tea I could find in the cupboard, and staggered toward the shop in the hope that maybe last night's ghost tantrum was a fluke.

It wasn't.

By the time I surveyed the full damage, I had counted two broken mirrors—small ones, thankfully, several witchy pun mugs in a heap like ceramic roadkill, and a scattering of broom-shaped pens stuck pointy end first into the ceiling tile.

I filled my lungs with the usual incense and the faint metallic tang of my own irritation.

"Okay," I muttered to no one in particular. "Let's try to make this look less like a crime scene."

I managed to right a table and rescue a box of velvet spell bags before I admitted the obvious: There was no way I could get the place customer-ready before Sissy showed up. And at this point, I wasn't sure it was even safe for my shop clerk—or anyone—to be here.

I pulled out my phone and tapped her number.

"Hey, Boo," she chirped, bright as ever.

"Listen," I said, "you don't need to come in today."

"Why not?"

Telling her about the ghost would probably freak her out. I thought fast. "Burst pipes."

There was a pause. "Again?"

"Afraid so."

"Merle fixed them before. Can't he do it again?"

70

"Probably, but he's got a lot on his plate. Don't worry. I'll pay you for the day."

"Really?"

It was the least I could do. "Of course. Enjoy yourself. It looks like a decent beach day."

"I've been wanting to visit the tide pools. Thanks, Boo. You sure you don't need help?"

"I'm sure," I said quickly. I wanted her to go to the tide pools and forget about the shop. At least for today. The fewer people tangled up in this mess, the better. "Enjoy your day off."

I hung up before she could ask more questions.

Then I did what I knew I had to do, as much as I hated to admit it. I called Del.

"Go ahead and bring in the big guns," I said when she answered.

My sister arrived thirty minutes later, with Opal, Jemma, and Willa close behind. Between Willa's bulky black sweater and corduroys, Opal's gauzy maroon pants, and Jemma's paisley-print top and broom skirt, there was no mistaking my friendly neighborhood garden witches had arrived.

Opal wrinkled her nose. "A ghost did this? She really let loose, didn't she?"

"Maybe she's frustrated," Jemma suggested, nudging a tipped-over "broom parking only" sign with her shoe.

"She's trying to communicate," Willa said, already pacing the floor with her eyes half-closed. "There's a message

71

here. Spirits often become impatient when their warnings go unheeded. Has she said anything?"

Del and I glanced at each other.

"Not exactly," I said. "But she wrote fire on the glass last night."

Three heads snapped my direction.

"You didn't say anything about a threat, Delphine," Willa scolded.

My sister stared at the ground.

"It wasn't a threat," I countered. "We think—I think—it has something to do with a story she was working on about the Channel Hotel fire. That's what she wanted to talk to Merle about and what I heard her asking Councilman Dodge about before she died."

"Before she was murdered, you mean," Willa said. "Let's be clear about what we're dealing with here."

"Point taken," I said. It didn't matter that my roots were gray, my hands ached with arthritis, and I needed a daily pill to keep my blood pressure under control, Willa could still make me feel like a pipsqueak girl with pigtails, if she tried.

"She was murdered," Willa repeated, "and maybe in her own way, she's trying to tell us why or by whom."

She was right, of course. We all seemed to agree on that. What no one seemed to agree on was what to do next, because the bickering began almost immediately.

"Can't we do a séance right now?" Jemma asked. "I don't want to come back at midnight. I have to get up early for a delivery at the gelato shop."

"I'm sorry if it inconveniences you," Willa snapped. "But the veil between worlds is thinnest at midnight. There's no way around that."

"Why do we need a séance at all?" Opal grumbled. "We could try a Ouija board or tarot cards."

"I don't have a Ouija board," I said.

"But you have tarot decks," Del said. "I should have thought of it last night. You could try speaking to her through the cards."

I glared at her. "You know I don't touch the cards anymore."

She crossed her arms. "Really? I thought you were over that dry spell."

It wasn't a dry spell, and she knew it. It was a betrayal, and it wasn't something a person just got over. She knew that too. That's probably why she was putting me on the spot in front of everyone.

"I already tried the pendulum, which I told you," I said. "It didn't work."

Opal walked between us and shook her hands like she could shake away the tension that had settled in the room. "There are other options. There have to be."

I waited for them to agree on something—anything. At least Kheppy wasn't here to toss in her two cents. She'd spent most of the night prowling outside, so I wasn't at all surprised she was too worn out to join us at the shop.

In the end, Willa won the debate and celebrated with an eye roll and an exasperated sigh. "If you want results, we need a proper séance. Spirits don't care about your sleep schedule. It's the best way to communicate with the other side."

"Speaking of communicating with the other side, where's Merle?" Jemma glanced around like he might be hiding behind the display of packaged costumes.

"Yeah," Opal added. "He talks to ghosts. Why didn't you call him?"

I stiffened. "He's busy."

There was a pause. Then, just as I turned to reorganize a shelf, I heard it—Opal's whisper, low and sharp.

"Busy? Or keeping a low profile because he's a suspect?"

Jemma murmured something back, too quiet to make out, but it didn't matter. My ears were already ringing. I clamped my mouth shut and pretended I hadn't heard a word.

"There's no use standing around here," I said, cutting through the tension. "If Fiona doesn't want to communicate, I need to find out what Councilman Dodge has planned for the Channel Hotel site. If she was killed because she was looking into it, I'd like to know who else is involved."

"You should go to the *Gazette* and talk to Cornelia," Del suggested. "She must know what her reporter was working on."

I shook my head. "Yesterday she nearly called the cops on me for giving away lemonade. Do you think she'd lift one finger to help me now?"

"Probably not," my sister said glumly.

"Definitely not," I corrected. "If I find out something, then I might be able to pry some details out of her. Or one of the other reporters."

Maybe even her minion Zelda, if I could get that woman alone.

"I'm going to start at the library," I said.

I couldn't think of a better place to begin a fact-finding mission, and for the first time that morning, everyone seemed to agree with me.

"While you're doing that," Del said, "I'll go home and make some calls. Maybe someone in our community knows what Fiona was up to. Cornelia might not help, but I'm sure the other elders will, if they know something."

I nodded. "Good thinking, Del."

Even if Neal Glory hadn't heard anything from the merfolk, he might have heard something from his clients at the hair salon. Same with Howard Collins at the hardware store.

"Just do me a favor and steer clear of the werewolves," I added. "They're too unpredictable."

And I was never sure where we stood with them, anyway.

"Sounds good." Del headed for the door.

Jemma glanced at the wall clock. "I hate to be a party pooper, but I need to get back to my shop before the lunch rush."

"Of course," I said. "Willa, do you want to join me at the library?"

She heaved a sigh. "I would, but Pickles didn't eat break-fast this morning. I should check on her and make sure she isn't coming down with something."

Willa's pug Pickles was her pride and joy, and as close to a child of her own as she'd ever gotten.

"Would you mind dropping me off on your way to the library, though?" she added. "It's on the way."

It was, and I didn't mind in the least.

"If you're looking for company, I'll go with you," Opal said.

Of all the garden witches in our circle, Opal was my least favorite—not because she was mean, exactly. Just a little smug. We'd known each other for years but had spent little one-on-one time together. I'd preferred it that way.

Del gave me a sympathetic look. She knew my feelings. Still, I couldn't turn Opal down without a good reason, so I forced a smile. "Sure. Let's do it."

The women gathered their things and drifted out of the shop. As Willa stepped onto the sidewalk, she turned back. "We need to meet back here at eleven-thirty tonight. No later."

Great. Something to look forward to.

Opal strode out, her wide-leg pants flapping behind her. She gave me a too-sweet smile. "Shall we?"

After the three of us said goodbye to my sister and Jemma, and I turned to lock the shop door behind me, I gave myself a silent pep talk. *Big girl pants, Boo. An hour of Opal won't be so bad. Probably.*

With Willa and Opal waiting for me, I paused to soak in the late-morning sun and the sweet smell of pastries and coffee drifting from the Scandinavian bakery across the street. It did nothing to calm my nerves.

"Fiona," I muttered under my breath, "if you can hear me, please, let's try for some peace and quiet today. No more messes, and I'll do what I can to help you. I promise."

There was no answer, but a sudden gust breezed by me. Then somewhere inside the shop, something shattered.

Opal glanced back. "Did you hear that?"

I nodded slowly.

So much for peace and quiet.

Chapter 10

Back Issues

My Karmann Ghia purred down the coastal road like a contented cat, but the silence inside the car was anything but soothing. After dropping Willa at home, it was only me and Opal in my cramped little car, and let's just say it was a cozy fit in the worst possible way.

I'd always gotten along with Opal well enough. Smug or not, I had to admit I appreciated her no-nonsense attitude and the way she always showed up for our gardening projects. But being alone with her was something else. She had strong opinions and zero hesitation about sharing them. I had a hunch this car ride would be no exception.

I cleared my throat as I fiddled with the air vent, even though my permanently stuck driver's-side window meant I never had a shortage of fresh air. "I'm surprised you have time for this. You're usually so busy."

Opal laughed lightly and smoothed a stray strand of her silky black hair, which today was pulled into a low bun. "I know. I should be at the senior center, but I told the director I needed some time off. They really can't complain since I'm a volunteer. I just need to be home by two, when Emma gets out of school."

Emma was Opal's eight-year-old granddaughter, who was in third grade now. Or was it fourth?

I nodded and tried to look interested. "I'm glad you were available. We so rarely get to spend time together, just the two of us."

Opal nodded after a brief pause. "Yes, it's nice. I thought you would appreciate the company. I read an article last week that said it's not good for older folks to go places alone. Too risky in case of a fall or health emergency."

I clamped my lips shut so the snarky comment on the tip of my tongue didn't fly out of my mouth. That woman was five years younger than me and hardly in a position to toss around the word old.

As I pulled into the library parking lot and slid into the first available space, I felt an almost embarrassing sense of relief. "Here we are," I said, maybe a little too brightly. I didn't care. I was just glad to escape that conversation and refocus on what mattered—why Fiona had fixated on the Channel Hotel fire, and how Merle might be involved.

Inside, the library smelled like old paper and pine-scented cleaner, a strangely comforting mix, and it was so quiet I could hear the electronic beeps as the librarian, Helen Velchick, ran a barcode scanner over the back covers of the books stacked beside her. When she saw me, her expression softened.

"Oh, Boo," she said, her voice low. "I heard what happened. I'm so sorry. It must have been such a shock."

Geez. Did everyone in Laguna Bay already know about the incident in the alley? Unless...

"You're talking about the murder investigation, right?" I asked.

Helen gave a short, confused shake of her head. "Of course. What else would I be talking about?"

I forced a small laugh. Helen was a normie—with no hint of psychic gifts or otherworldly senses—but she was smart. I wouldn't be surprised if she knew more than she let on about this town's supernatural secrets. Still, I was glad she hadn't heard about my ghostly guest. Not yet, anyway.

"Sorry. It's been a long day," I added, which was putting it mildly.

Helen's eyes flicked to the wall clock. It was only ten in the morning, but she was kind enough not to mention it. "May I help you find something?"

I scratched my head, realizing I didn't know where to start. Beside me, Opal was digging something out from under a fingernail. When she caught me watching, she raised one dark eyebrow as if to say, "Don't look at me."

No help there. Why wasn't I surprised?

"Where do you keep old editions of the *Gazette*?" I asked. Starting with Fiona's previous articles seemed the most logical move.

"We keep copies from the past twelve months in the news archive room at the end of the hall." Helen gestured to the corridor on the right. "We digitize everything older than that and put it online."

"Then I'll start with the archive room," I said, my voice firmer now that I had a plan.

Opal followed me past rows of community bulletin boards and half-occupied study tables. Tucked behind a frosted glass door, the news archive room was really more of a glorified closet. I pushed it open and breathed in the musty scent of old newsprint.

The place was cramped, with tables pushed against each of the three walls and old newspapers stacked on every surface. At the closest table, I found yesterday's edition. A smile tugged at my lips when I saw Merle's picture on the front page, all broad-shouldered confidence as he posed with the other two mayoral candidates.

"Does he still have a chance?" Opal asked, startling me. She was peering at the photo over my shoulder, close enough that I could smell the breath mint that was working hard to cover the smell of her morning coffee.

"What do you mean?" I asked, eyes narrowing.

"With the election." She smirked like it should have been obvious.

"Of course he does." My tone was sharper than I'd intended, but it was the truth. And it would've been the same even if she'd been referring to the other thing—the more personal meaning that had flickered through my mind.

Opal's lips pressed into a thin line. "I just think people will wonder why he was the first person the police talked to after they found the body."

"That doesn't mean anything." Every muscle in my body tensed. "You know Merle. He wouldn't hurt a fly, let alone a person."

She didn't answer, just reached over and flipped the page. "Oh, look. There's a nice article about last week's art festival. You should think about participating in that. It would be great for your shop."

Seriously? Did she really think people who went to those things to support the town's talented artists would be interested in the Boo-tique's crystal balls and witch kitsch?

"Thanks," I said, "but I'm not everyone's cup of tea."

"You never know," she said breezily and turned the page.

I didn't know if I was more irritated by her suggestion, her comment about Merle, or the fact she wouldn't even let me finish reading before she flipped to a new page. I grabbed another issue and handed it to her. "We'll get through this faster if we split the stack."

If she realized I was trying to get rid of her, she didn't show it. She took the paper, spread it out on the next table, and started to read. A second later, her head popped up. "What should I be looking for?"

"I don't know," I said, trying not to sound impatient. "Anything that seems suspicious or out of place."

She let out a frustrated sigh but didn't argue, plopped one elbow on the table, and rested her cheek in her palm as she focused on her task.

I scanned my issue for articles by Fiona Richards. If she'd been digging up dirt on the city council, maybe I'd find something relevant. Or maybe something about the Channel Hotel site.

I was halfway through my fifth issue when I realized I hadn't seen anything relevant. In fact, I hadn't seen much of anything at all—no city hall scandals, no exposés, and not a single article by Fiona Richards.

As I combed through the stack again more slowly, something else jumped out. This wasn't just Cornelia flexing her Gatekeeper muscle. Pages were missing. Entire issues, in fact.

"You don't happen to have last Thursday's paper, do you?" I asked Opal.

She glanced up. "No. Have you seen the prices of the old cottages on the bluffs? A one-bedroom is going for—"

"That's fascinating," I said through clenched teeth. "But not exactly relevant."

Opal huffed and rolled her eyes. "If you didn't want my help, you should have said so."

I ignored her and walked back to the front desk. The librarian was still there, arranging books on a rolling cart.

"Hey, Helen, I noticed some copies are missing. Any idea where they are?"

Her head popped up like a prairie dog. "I'd almost forgotten. Councilman Dodge requested some back issues to research an environmental impact report he's putting together for the planning commission."

"An environmental what now?" I asked.

"Sorry—city-hall jargon. It's an assessment of the environmental effects of a proposed project."

That was interesting, but something still didn't sit right with me. "I thought back issues were reference-only. No checkouts allowed."

Helen's nose wrinkled. "That's true, technically. But he said he was on a tight deadline and really needed them, so we bent the rules a teensy bit."

"When did this happen exactly?" I asked, fighting to keep my tone even, though the whole thing smelled fishy.

"A couple of days ago," she said. "I'm sure he'll bring them back soon. I can give you a call when they're returned."

That would have been fine if I'd been in the mood to wait. But I wasn't. And since I was pretty sure anything I was hoping to find was in those missing issues, I made a new plan.

"Thanks, but that won't be necessary. I'll head over to city hall and see if I can persuade the councilman to let me have a look."

Even if he was trying to hide something, he wouldn't dare risk drawing suspicion by refusing a request from a concerned constituent—especially one like me.

"You're going to city hall?" Opal asked.

I hadn't realized she'd followed me to the front desk, but there she was, standing behind me, her eyes bright with an eagerness that was both endearing and exasperating.

"I can take you home first," I said. "You don't have to come."

Truth be told, ambushing the councilman wasn't exactly an adventure I wanted to share, but my subtle hint didn't land.

"Of course I'll come!" she said, her grin widening. "This is so exciting! We're like Cagney and Lacey, or Rosemary and Thyme, or..."

She paused, tapping a finger to her lips as she tried to think of another famous crime-solving duo.

While she deliberated, I stared at the ceiling and wondered—again—why I never learned to keep my plans to myself.

Chapter 11

City Hall

THE AIR IN THE Laguna Bay city hall waiting room carried that faint chemical tang of hand sanitizer, layered with the receptionist's perfume—a cloying mix of gardenia and boredom. Opal sat beside me on a chunky metal chair, serene to the point of sedation, while I tried not to grind my molars into dust.

We'd been waiting long enough for me to memorize every motivational poster on the walls. My foot tapped a steady beat against the floor as I tried not to notice the receptionist's constant glare. And Opal? She seemed on the verge of falling asleep.

The longer we waited, the more I regretted bringing her along. Confronting the councilman about the missing newspaper issues had felt like a solid plan back at the library—but now, I wasn't so sure. If he were hiding something, he wouldn't just hand them over. And if I pressed the issue, I'd have to explain why.

Was I ready to make that kind of accusation?

If I was about to make a fool of myself, I'd rather do it without an audience, especially one guaranteed to report every detail to my sister and the entire garden witch grapevine.

"You know," I said in what I hoped was a casual tone, "if you'd rather go home, I can drop you off and come back."

She beamed at me, completely missing the hint. "Don't be silly. We're in this together. We're a team."

Great. Like it or not, she'd have a front-row seat to my almost-certain humiliation.

The receptionist's phone buzzed. She picked it up, but instead of her usual, "Laguna Bay City Council offices" greeting, her voice lowered to a whisper. I caught snippets. "I don't think so, Councilman. Yes, that's right. Okay."

After she hung up, a door at the end of the hall opened with an ominous squeal. Councilman Tom Dodge stepped out with a wide, undoubtedly practiced smile. As he approached, he buttoned his navy blazer over his crisp white dress shirt and red tie before running a finger over his narrow mustache.

"Hello," he said warmly as he reached the lobby. "So sorry to keep you waiting. My meeting ran long."

His voice was sweet as honey, but I wasn't buying that jovial demeanor for a minute.

The receptionist rose from her desk, smoothed her skirt, and came around to make introductions.

"Councilman Dodge, this is Boo Boudreaux and Opal Uttari, representing…" She looked at me expectantly, as if waiting for me to fill in the blank.

"Representing myself," I said, keeping my tone polite but firm. "A concerned citizen."

The councilman shook my hand. When it was Opal's turn, her cheeks went pink. Whether it was flattery or fluster, I couldn't tell. Maybe both.

The man's handshake was firm but brief, and his smile never wavered. "A personal matter, you said? Funny, as Merle Foster's campaign manager, I thought you might be here to tell me he was dropping out of the race. That would be such a shame but certainly understandable under the circumstances."

My jaw tensed. "I can assure you, Merle isn't dropping out of anything."

"Oh, of course," he said lightly, but his eyes didn't match the tone. "I didn't mean to imply anything to the contrary."

He was a good actor, but I'd seen enough politicians in my time to know when they were playing games.

"This doesn't have anything to do with the election," I said. "I'm here because Helen Velchick at the library told me you have some of their copies of the *Gazette*. I was hoping I could take a look at them."

The councilman's smile faltered. Only for a second, but it was enough to tell me I'd struck a nerve. "Helen must be mistaken," he said, his voice suddenly cool.

Laguna Bay's head librarian was many things, but rarely was she mistaken. I leaned back. "Really? She said you requested them for a report regarding the old Channel Hotel site."

He stiffened and glanced at the receptionist. "Are you aware of any request for *Gazette* back issues?" he asked.

The poor young woman looked like she wanted to crawl under her desk. "No, sir."

Opal chimed in. "Oh, Boo, there's obviously been a misunderstanding. I'm sure the councilman wouldn't forget something like that."

I shot her a look. Whose side was she on? I wanted to ask, but Tom Dodge was my focus.

"That's interesting, Councilman," I said, "because I have to wonder if your request for those back issues had anything to do with Fiona Richards' stories accusing you and your council colleagues of accepting gifts and donations you didn't report. Or maybe it had something to do with the argument I heard between you and that reporter outside my shop yesterday."

His eyes went cold. "Perhaps we should speak about this in my office. If you'll come with me."

Opal and I followed him into an office filled with mahogany furniture, plaques, and framed certificates and grip-and-grin photos with local business leaders.

When he offered us seats, Opal settled into a cushy chair near his desk. I remained on my feet. So did he.

"I'd like to know what you're implying," he said, staring at me.

The simmering anger in his voice emboldened me. I squared my shoulders and met his gaze. "I heard Fiona ask you about a project on the old Channel Hotel site. You seemed eager to avoid the topic, though."

He responded with a dismissive laugh. "I support many projects in this town. But I have to wonder if you're implying I had something to do with her death."

"I'm not implying anything," I said. "If you've conveniently forgotten about those back issues, though, maybe it's because they contain something you didn't want her or anyone else to see."

His glare turned hostile. "You raise an interesting question, Ms. Boudreaux. Let me ask one in return. Why would Merle Foster's campaign manager come to my office to threaten me while he's the one sitting in jail?"

My blood ran cold. "Merle isn't in jail. But since we're talking about Fiona's murder—where were you when she was killed?"

He appeared genuinely rattled, but only for a moment. That oily politician's grin was back in an instant. "I don't even know when that was," he said.

Sure he didn't.

"It was after the town hall," I said. "Sometime between four and six in the evening."

He shrugged. "I was visiting shopkeepers. Shaking hands and asking for votes. If you were a real campaign manager, you would have made sure Merle was doing the same."

"Is that so?" I asked, my voice sharp. "How many bribes—excuse me, undeclared gifts—did Fiona uncover that went to you, Councilman? Seems like a good reason to want a reporter silenced, if you ask me."

He stepped closer and lowered his voice. "Fiona was a troublemaker. An ambitious little twit. Just ask her boss. I lodged a complaint, and it was being taken care of. I didn't have to kill her. Any story she wrote about the Channel Hotel site wouldn't have anything to do with me."

The door to his office opened then, and Eleanor Voss stuck her head in, all perfect hair and shiny smile. "Tom, dear, so sorry to interrupt. Will you be coming by the house tonight to review plans for tomorrow's election night party?"

He looked at me, then back at Eleanor. "Yes, of course. I'll stop by once I'm finished here." Then he went to her, whispered something that made her smile brighten, and shut the door behind her.

When he turned back to Opal and me, he pulled himself up to his full height, all five feet seven inches of it. "I believe we're done here. As you can see, I'm quite busy. Forgive me if I don't see you out." He opened the door and stood beside it, waiting for us to leave.

"Let me get this straight," I said dryly. "You're refusing to let me see the back issues you took from the library?"

"I told you, I don't have them. Good day, Ms. Boudreaux, Ms. Uttari."

Opal popped up and thanked the councilman profusely before hurrying to the door.

I stared at her gushing display. Why was she kissing up to that creep?

"Good day, Councilman," I grumbled on my way out.

As we headed out to the parking lot, Opal was practically buzzing. "That was certainly something!" she gushed. "Do you think they're dating?"

"Who?" I asked, my mind still reeling over the confrontation. My gut told me the councilman was guilty.

"The councilman and Eleanor Voss," she sputtered as we neared my car.

"Dodge and Eleanor? I don't know. That's not really the issue."

She muttered something under her breath as I unlocked the passenger side, but I wasn't listening. I was watching the councilman hustle out of the office from a side door. He glanced around as though he were looking for someone, then skipped down the steps and got into a silver Mercedes-Benz parked in a reserved spot.

I hurried Opal into the car, slid behind the wheel, and followed him out, keeping just enough distance not to be noticed.

He took a quick left, then another, and I did the same as my heart thudded in my chest.

"You should have gone right back there," Opal whined. "Did you forget how to get to my house?"

"Oh, yeah. Sorry," I said. No point telling her I wasn't taking her home yet. I was stalking the councilman.

I made a couple more turns, and Opal still didn't know what I was doing or where I was going.

"Boo, it might be better if you head up to Forest Avenue and then turn back," she said.

I could hear the concern in her voice. She probably thought I was having a senior moment, which was fine by me. I touched my forehead and pretended to be confused. "You're right. What was I thinking?"

Luckily, Councilman Dodge didn't make any other turns. I figured he was probably heading to the main canyon road that would take him out to Eleanor's place, because even though I didn't say it to Opal, there definitely seemed to be something between those two. It made sense. An available, middle-aged woman with cash to burn was probably a sketchy politician's ideal date.

I was so convinced he was on his way to see Eleanor that when he swerved into a parking space just before we reached Forest Avenue, it was too late for me to turn onto a different road before I passed him. I prayed he didn't notice me behind the wheel.

After we passed, I watched through the rearview mirror and saw him leave his car and jog across the street.

But where was he going? There wasn't a restaurant there or even a place to grab coffee. That building held a nail salon, an after-school tutoring company, and the offices of the *Laguna Bay Gazette*.

Oh.

That could be a problem.

Chapter 12

The Gazette

By the third loop around the *Laguna Bay Gazette*, I was feeling less like a concerned citizen and more like a nosy ex with too much time on her hands. Councilman Tom Dodge's silver Mercedes-Benz was still parked on the street, glinting in the noontime sun, all polish and ego. My palms were sweating on the wheel, and my stomach churned—a queasy mix of nerves and the leftover gumbo I'd had for breakfast.

At least Opal wasn't here to witness my descent into stalker madness or question my methods. As soon as I'd realized the councilman was visiting the newspaper's office, I'd rushed to drop her off at home, refused her offer of tea and freshly baked cookies, and hurried back.

The Mercedes hadn't budged, which meant I hadn't missed anything. Not that I knew what I expected to find. The councilman could be visiting the *Gazette* for any number of reasons. It didn't mean he had killed Fiona to stop a story—but it didn't prove he hadn't, either.

Something about Tom Dodge didn't sit right. He was hiding something. I could feel it.

The fourth time around the block, a battered pickup truck pulled away from a shady spot nearby, and I saw my chance. I slid in, cut the engine, and slumped down in the driver's seat to watch the *Gazette*'s front door. The ocean breeze drifted through the open window, the salty air mixing with the faint whiff of car exhaust.

Five minutes ticked by. Then ten. I could see my reflection in the rearview mirror—dark circles under my eyes, electric blue hair frizzing at the part from the humidity—and wondered what in the world I was going to do if I actually saw Tom come out. Arrest him with my glare? Good luck with that.

A couple in bright beach shirts and flip-flops, hauling folding chairs and a cooler toward the shore, paused on the sidewalk to give me the stink eye as if I were up to no good. I smiled sweetly and waved, hoping—for probably the first time in my life—to look like nothing more than a harmless old lady.

It must have worked because the pair crossed the street and continued toward the boardwalk, away from my sad excuse of a stakeout.

I figured I'd better do something before someone called me in as a suspicious person, so I stepped out into the warm sunshine and made my way to the *Gazette*'s door.

Inside, the place was quiet. The lobby walls were lined with framed front pages from Laguna Bay's past, and a faint whiff of musty newsprint lingered in the air. Zelda Harcourt sat at the front desk, her headset slightly askew as she took a call. She didn't look up when I walked in—which gave me a moment to take it all in.

The front office was unusually quiet. Through the glass wall, I could see the newsroom beyond—neat rows of empty metal desks stretching toward the far end, where the publisher's corner office sat with its door shut tight. If Cornelia Sloane was in the building, she'd be in there. And I had a feeling Councilman Dodge was too.

When Zelda finished her call, she turned her attention to me. Her professional smile slipped away. "How can I help you, Ms. Boudreaux?" she asked, tapping her pen on the desk.

"Where is everybody?" I glanced around at all the empty desks.

Zelda scoffed. "Ms. Sloane gave people the day off to grieve. I doubt that's what they're doing, though, considering no one even liked Fiona. But whatever." She rolled her eyes.

I swallowed hard. I hadn't exactly liked Fiona Richards when I'd met her, either. Apparently I wasn't alone. "Of course," I murmured. "Losing a colleague like that must have hit the office pretty hard."

Zelda tilted her head like she wasn't sure if I was being sarcastic. I wasn't.

"How can I help you?" she asked with zero enthusiasm.

"I'd like to see your back issues." I figured I may as well check the missing ones while I kept an eye on the councilman.

Zelda's brows arched. "Would you like a particular page or the full edition? We sell them both ways."

My mouth dropped open. "I have to buy them?"

"Well, yeah," she said. "That's how it works. We're not a library. If you want to read them for free, the library stocks old issues."

I was about to mention that I'd already tried the library when the corner office door opened and Tom Dodge strolled out, calm as ever. He adjusted the cuffs of his blazer with a Cheshire-cat grin, like he'd just sealed a deal. Cornelia followed close behind.

The moment she saw me, her sophisticated smile twitched. After a lifetime of knowing that vampire, I could read an encyclopedia's worth of meaning in that twitch. None of it was good.

"Consider it done, Tom," Cornelia cooed in her velvety voice. "Don't worry about a thing."

Tom gave her a toothy grin and turned to go.

Zelda jumped in. "Are you still interested in the back issues?"

The councilman heard her and shook his head. "Still at it, Ms. Boudreaux?" His voice was low and mocking. "Well, good luck. You're going to need it."

What a jerk.

I watched him push through the glass door, wishing I could think of a snappy comeback to throw back at him.

"Will you excuse me for a moment?" Zelda asked and grabbed a garment bag hanging from a cabinet door. She hustled it back to the publisher's office before I could re-spond.

"Ms. Sloane, I have your dress for the election party," Zelda said. "I had it dry-cleaned, just like you asked."

I craned my neck to see into the office. Zelda was practically bowing as she handed over the dress, while Cornelia held it up with her usual air of disdain. For a second, I wondered if vampire glamour was at play. Zelda's fawning was so over-the-top, it bordered on bizarre.

Cornelia said something I couldn't hear, laid the dress across the back of a chair, and waved Zelda away with a mumbled word.

Zelda practically tripped over her own feet getting back to the reception desk, her cheeks flushed pink.

Cornelia remained at her open office door, glaring at me. "If you're here with an excuse for why Merle missed his candidate interview, don't bother," she said, her voice slicing through the air. "Reschedule for this afternoon, or he'll be removed from consideration."

"Fine," I said coolly. I hadn't even known he'd missed the interview. Great. As bad as I was at stakeouts, apparently I was even worse at managing campaigns.

As Zelda slipped behind the reception desk, I said, "I'll come back for those issues. I'm sure you're busy packing up Fiona's things."

I figured that would earn me a quick exit. No such luck.

Zelda scoffed. "What's to pack? She never kept anything here. Too paranoid someone might scoop her exclusives."

"News is a tough business," I said evenly, though I was seething inside. I was mad at myself for not making sure Merle made it to his interview, and even madder at that arrogant weasel, Tom Dodge. And Cornelia? Don't get me started. What was she doing cozying up to that arrogant little normie, anyway?

Still, I wasn't about to shell out a chunk of cash for back issues until I knew what I was looking for. "I need to narrow down the dates," I said, aiming for professional but knowing I was falling short. "I'll get back to you."

I pushed out the door and into the sunlight. The early afternoon glow shimmered off the ocean in the distance, and the breeze carried the scent of salt and tropical sunscreen. Two surfers wandered barefoot down the sidewalk, boards tucked beneath their arms, sun-bleached hair gleaming like sea glass.

I paused at the curb, taking it all in—this bright, bustling beach town that seemed so easygoing on the surface. But I knew better.

I drew a deep breath, trying to quiet the churn in my chest.

Was I in over my head? This wasn't just about clearing Merle's name anymore. Councilman Dodge was involved. I was sure of it. Maybe Cornelia Sloane as well.

Whatever Fiona had been investigating had ruffled some dangerous feathers and possibly gotten her killed. I didn't want to risk our supernatural community being discovered, but I also didn't want to risk being the killer's next victim. I had to tread carefully.

My phone buzzed in my purse, yanking me from my thoughts. I pulled it out to see a message from Delphine: *"Boo, where are you? Call me asap."*

A shiver ran down my spine. Del never texted like that. My pulse picked up, and I glanced at the *Gazette*'s windows one more time before heading for my car.

As I slid behind the wheel, I couldn't shake the feeling that something had shifted. I'd hoped to connect some dots and somehow wound up with a whole new set of them—and not a single answer in sight.

Chapter 13

Hocus Focus

THE SCENT OF ROASTED tomato salsa filled the kitchen as I spooned it generously over my avocado quesadilla, savoring that smoky tang that always felt like a tiny personal victory. In Southern California, everyone has a salsa recipe—some sweet, some fiery—but mine had the perfect zing. It was the one thing I made better than Delphine. She could probably outdo me if she tried, but she was gracious enough to let me keep this win.

I thumbed through the stack of mail Delphine had moved to the counter. When I came to the envelope with the New Orleans postmark, the one I'd noticed and ignored the day before, I pushed the whole stack aside. I couldn't deal with whatever that envelope held then, and I still couldn't now. Not today.

"Del, I'm telling you, he's up to something." My voice was muffled as I took another mouthful of the creamy avocado and the spicy salsa, a welcome distraction from the morning's frustrations.

Delphine stood at the sink, scrubbing dirt off her forearms, the area left unprotected by her gardening gloves. She still had on her gardening hat, but that skeptical squint under its wide brim told me she didn't buy it. "He was probably there on election business. You said yourself Cornelia is interviewing all the mayoral candidates."

I licked a bit of tomato from my finger and watched her. "If you'd seen that arrogant look on his face, you'd know he was practically daring me to accuse him of something."

Del turned off the faucet and faced me, water droplets catching the light on her sun-kissed arms as she reached for a dishtowel.

"You didn't, did you?"

"Of course not," I said—though I'd definitely considered it.

Kheppy leaped onto the table, her fluffy tail flicking back and forth as she sniffed at my plate. I pulled it closer, giving her a look. "Since when do you eat quesadillas?"

"I do not," Kheppy said with disdain. "But I would like something."

Delphine laughed softly and opened the refrigerator. "I'm not surprised. You slept through breakfast. I was worried you might be getting sick. You never miss a meal."

Kheppy seemed sluggish, but she tried to rally. "I feel fine. Just tired."

I frowned. "I heard you slip out around midnight. What were you up to at that hour?"

We'd had a doggy door installed in the back so she could come and go as she pleased, but she rarely went out so late.

Kheppy yawned. "I lost the time."

"You mean you lost track of time?" I said, watching her closely.

"If you say so," Kheppy muttered, but she turned her attention to the small plate of tuna Delphine set in front of her. She tucked into it, but with less gusto than usual. I made a mental note to keep an eye on her. I'd never known her to get sick—and I'd known her my entire life—but I suppose it was possible, even for an immortal cat like her.

I dragged my quesadilla through more salsa. "You've been staying out late a lot lately," I said lightly. "What's going on? Do you have a boyfriend?"

Kheppy didn't bother lifting her head from the plate. "I have no boyfriend. Do you?"

The look she gave me could have cut glass. My cheeks warmed. "I wouldn't call Merle a boyfriend."

"But he's not not a boyfriend, right?" Delphine pressed, with a mischievous twinkle in her eye. She'd been needling me about Merle for days, but I wasn't ready to admit anything.

Sensing my discomfort, she switched topics. "So, the councilman. Why were you at the *Gazette*, anyway? I thought you and Opal were going to the library."

"We were, and we did," I said, taking another bite of the toasty tortilla. "But when I tried to look up Fiona's old stories to get a sense of what she may have been investigating about the Channel Hotel site, there were a bunch of issues missing. Helen told me Tom Dodge requested them, so I went to city hall to ask if I could see them."

Del leaned against the counter, her hat drooping a little. "You went to city hall too? Where haven't you been today?"

I shrugged. "We weren't there long. Dodge was downright rude when I asked to see those issues."

"Rude?" she asked. "For no reason at all?"

I knew what she was getting at. "Not a good reason. I can tell you that much. Ask Opal."

Del sighed. "So, because the councilman wouldn't hand over a few newspapers, that means he's involved with Fiona's murder?"

Sure, it sounded a little silly when she said it like that.

"You didn't see him," I said. "He got mad and shifty. There's something off about him."

My eyes drifted to the counter, where my *Hocus Focus* notebook peeked out from under a half-finished grocery list and a coupon for cat treats. Del had given it to me last year to help me get organized. I'd meant to use it for to-do lists and important reminders but had never gotten around to it.

Maybe now was the time.

I grabbed the notebook and a pen from the junk drawer and flipped to a clean page.

Tom Dodge, I wrote. Then underneath: *Cornelia Sloane*.

"What are you doing?" Delphine leaned over my shoulder for a peek.

"Getting organized," I said. "Because I'll bet there's more going on between those two than the newspaper's endorsement. I mean, why did he run straight to the *Gazette* after Opal and I left his office?"

I jotted that down too.

Del raised an eyebrow. "A better question is, why did you run to the *Gazette*?"

I pushed the notebook aside and polished off the last of my crispy, gooey quesadilla.

But Del wasn't done with me. She crossed her arms, her expression fixed in determined sister mode.

"You followed him, didn't you?" she said finally.

"Maybe," I said, trying for nonchalance.

Kheppy looked up from her tuna. "I told you, Delphine," she said.

My sister removed her hat and hung it on the hook by the back door. "You're right. You win," she said with a sigh.

"Win what?" I asked, looking from Delphine to Kheppy.

"It's not important," Del said airily.

Kheppy sniffed and rubbed one white paw across her mouth. "Your sister said you would not get involved in this investigation. That you had learned your lesson last time and would leave it to the police. I told her you wouldn't be able to resist. You can't even walk away from a jigsaw puzzle until every piece has found its place."

"That's not true," I muttered. But it was true. At least the part about the jigsaw puzzles. Del had banned them from the house years ago because I spent hours obsessing over them.

The looks I got from Kheppy and Del told me they knew it was true too.

I took my plate to the sink and scraped the last bits of salsa down the garbage disposal, then washed the dish. The warm water felt good on my fingers, easing the arthritis that was acting up in my thumb. It was a nice, if momentary, distraction from the swirling questions.

I put the plate on the drying rack and turned to them. "As much as I'd love to sit here all day and gab, I've got things to do, people to see, and mysteries to solve." My voice was light, but there was an edge to it even I could hear.

Delphine and Kheppy exchanged frustrated looks.

"Boo," Del began.

I cut her off with a raised hand. "Don't," I said softly. "I know you're concerned. But I can't sit around and do nothing."

I grabbed my phone off the counter and tried Merle's number, but it went straight to voicemail—again. I'd already left a message, so I hung up with a sigh. Why hadn't he called me back?

A wave of unease rolled through me. Merle wasn't the type to ignore me—even if he was mad—not unless something was seriously wrong. My pulse quickened, and I took a moment to steady my breath.

I pushed back from the counter and scooped up the notebook, pen, and my worn denim jacket in one swift motion.

"I'm going to see Merle," I said, keeping my voice steady—even though inside I was coiled tighter than a spring.

Delphine's brow wrinkled. "Maybe you should go to the police first. You could tell that nice Detective Platt about your concerns. Tell him everything you've told Kheppy and me."

"I'm sure that would go over well," I said, heading toward the door. "He already thinks I'm a few cat hairs short of a furball."

"He does not," Del said, but her voice wavered. We both knew the detective thought I was an eccentric old woman who ran a spooky little shop. "But if you insist, then at least be careful."

"I will," I said. And I would be.

She watched as I grabbed my purse and keys. I could see it in her eyes—she wanted to stop me, but she didn't. She knew better than anyone that once I set my mind to something, I wouldn't quit until it was done.

Chapter 14

Backyard Barbecue

SOMETHING WAS WRONG. I knew it the moment I stepped onto Merle Foster's driveway and caught the scent of smoke and lighter fluid in the air.

His truck was parked in front of the garage in its usual way—slightly askew to keep the back end out of the street—so I knew he was home. But nobody answered when I knocked. I tried the doorbell, then peeked through the window. Still no sign of him.

The smoky smell grew stronger, so I followed my nose around the side of the house. The gate to his backyard was latched, but I could see through a gap between the slats. He was there.

Merle stood at his portable charcoal grill, a metal poker in one hand, stabbing at a roaring flame. On the picnic table beside him sat a stack of manila folders.

"What are you doing, Merle Foster?" I yelled.

He jumped, spun around, and stared at the fence like a kid caught with his hand in the cookie jar—if that cookie jar were full of incriminating documents.

After a moment, he shuffled over and unlatched the gate. "You shouldn't be here, Boo."

"Why not?" I peered around his broad shoulders at the blaze. "Please tell me you aren't doing what I think you're doing."

"It's not your concern," he shot back.

I glared at him, but he didn't back down. I shrugged. "Cornelia said you didn't show up for your candidate interview at the *Gazette* this morning, and if you don't get in there this afternoon, she'll pull you from consideration." I brushed past him before he could stop me. "But I have to admit, at the moment I'm more interested in this bonfire of yours."

He rubbed the back of his neck, looking guilty as sin. "Just some overdue housekeeping."

"Really?" I walked up to the leaning tower of folders. "This doesn't look like housekeeping." I didn't want to say it looked like he was destroying evidence, because I didn't want to believe it. And I definitely didn't want him thinking I did.

As he moved up beside me, he released a long, slow breath. "I may as well tell you. You're going to find out, anyway."

I was prepared for an angry Merle. Even a frustrated Merle. This was something else. "Find out what?"

He dragged a hand over his face and looked everywhere but at me. Finally, he answered. "I've done things, Boo. Things I'm not proud of. I think they're coming back to haunt me."

After a beat, he glanced at the empty air beside him and rolled his eyes. "She knows I mean figuratively," he muttered.

I crossed my arms. "Rupert's here?"

Merle nodded slightly, his eyes never leaving the space beside the table.

"Hi, Rupert," I said to his spirit companion. "May Merle and I have some privacy?"

I caught Merle's slight nod before he said, "He's gone. It's just us."

"Good," I said, deciding to believe him. "So, what is all this?"

I glanced down at the folders and froze. The top one was labeled *Channel Hotel Appraisal*. Beneath it sat a thicker folder marked *Channel Hotel Correspondence*.

A chill shot down my spine, slicing through the warm afternoon air.

"Why do you have these?" I asked, the words sharper than I'd meant them to be.

Merle didn't answer. He closed his eyes and shook his head.

I stepped closer. Only charcoal bricks and the grate sat in the barbecue's basin. No files. Or at least no evidence of them. "Did you have anything to do with the Channel Hotel fire?"

My stomach clenched at the words. I didn't want to say them. I certainly didn't want to believe them. But I had to know.

Merle's shoulders sagged. He shook his head slowly.

Relief hit me like a wave, but it didn't last. His expression twisted with pain. He finally looked up.

"Do you really think I'd be capable of that?" he asked, his voice low. Hurt stewed behind his words.

He was right. *How could I think such a thing?*

I felt a pang of shame. "I don't know what to think, Merle. This whole mess has me so twisted up. Why are you out here? What is all this?"

He mumbled something, but not to me. I couldn't hear it, but from the tilt of his head and the weight in his sigh, I guessed Rupert was back. Maybe he'd never left.

"Fine," Merle said finally, his voice rough. "I wasn't involved in the fire. I didn't know it was going to happen. But I knew Maureen Calvert."

That name shattered my thoughts like a glass hitting tile.

Maureen was the woman who ran the Channel Hotel, the one who had fled after the fire—and the deaths.

"Were you two involved?" I asked before I could stop myself.

He frowned, confused, then realized what I meant. "No, not like that. She hired me."

"To do what?" My gut twisted.

He ran a hand through his hair. "She said she wanted an appraisal for her insurance company, but I knew that wasn't right. I didn't care. Business had been slow, and I needed the work. I didn't ask questions." He looked at me, guilt plainly etched on his face.

"Did you tell the police?"

He shook his head. "I figured an investigator would come knocking eventually. I assumed someone would mention the appraisal. But no one ever did. The more time went by, the more it seemed like people just wanted to move on. I let them."

He looked down at the smoldering coals.

I narrowed my eyes. "So, now you're going to burn the evidence?"

"What else can I do? If I turn it over now, it'll look like I knew what she was planning. I didn't, Boo. I had no idea she was going to burn that place down. I thought she intended to put it on the market."

"But you have to tell the police what you know," I said. "It's the right thing to do."

"I'll lose the election," he said as he stared into the flames.

He was probably right, and that was a shame. It still didn't change anything.

"You have to do it," I said gently. "This isn't you. You're not the guy who hides the truth. You're better than this."

He laughed bitterly. "Am I? I haven't done anything for so long. Too long. Maybe it's too late now."

I stepped closer and put my hand on his shoulder. His plaid shirt was warm from the fire and the afternoon sun. He smelled faintly of smoke and soap. I looked up at him, right into those steel-blue eyes.

"It's never too late to do the right thing. And if you weren't the man I thought you were, that stack would already be cinders. You'd have done it years ago. But you didn't. Because there's too much good in you, Merle. I know it. I know Rupert knows it too. It's time you believed it."

For a moment, he looked like he was working on an excuse. Then his eyes softened, and he nodded, just barely.

That's when my phone buzzed in my back pocket.

I pulled it out and saw Del's name on the screen. I answered with a quick, "Hey."

"Tempeh tacos or tofu cutlets?" she asked.

"Are those my only choices?"

"With everything that's been going on, I didn't get to the grocery store. It's all I have in the fridge. So, tempeh or tofu?"

I sighed. Then an idea struck. "Actually, I meant to call you. I'm with Merle, and we were just heading to the Beachside Café for a late lunch. Want me to bring you something?"

Merle looked confused, but it was the silence on the other end of the line that worried me. Then my sister said, "Last time I was there, Chef Glen said he was going to add a new vegan cheesecake to his menu. I wouldn't mind trying it."

"You got it! I'll bring you home a slice." Heck, I'd bring her the whole fake-cheese cheesecake if it meant I wouldn't have to choke down anything that involved tempeh or tofu. "Should I bring something home for Kheppy?"

"There's a bit of boiled chicken in the fridge from yesterday. I'll put it out, but she's been asleep on your bed since you left. Should I wake her up?"

These new night-owl hours were starting to take a toll. "No, let her sleep," I said. "If she's hungry, she'll let you know."

Kheppy had never been a suffer-in-silence kind of cat.

"All right," Del said. "Will you be home before the séance, or should I meet you at the shop?"

I'd almost forgotten about our midnight appointment with my shop's phantom visitor. I checked my watch. It was still hours away, but I was already feeling like it had been a long day. All I really wanted to do was crawl into my comfy jammies and curl up on the couch with a good book.

Then again, maybe it was just low blood sugar. Once I ate, I might get a second wind.

"Probably best if we met there," I said.

After I hung up with Delphine, Merle tilted his head and asked, "Got a hot date tonight?"

I still hadn't told him about Fiona haunting the Boo-tique, and now didn't feel like the right time, either. He had enough on his plate with the election and this whole Channel Hotel mess. It could wait.

I turned to him and asked, a little sheepishly, "Feel like joining me for a late lunch at Beachside Café?"

"Sure," he said. When he chuckled softly, I knew things between us would be okay. Maybe not perfect, but I didn't need perfect. I just needed my friend.

"Unless there are other secrets you want to get off your chest," I added, only half kidding.

"No, I'm good."

"As far as I'm concerned," I added, "you're pretty great."

His cheeks flushed before he closed the barbecue's lid to extinguish the flames and scooped up the stack of folders. "I should probably put these away before we head out."

I considered asking him to bring the files because there might be a clue or two buried in them, but when I noticed he was wearing his Vote for Merle baseball cap instead of his usual cowboy hat, it hit me. I'd been so wrapped up in playing detective, I'd let my campaign manager duties slide. Again.

That had to change before the other candidates ran circles around us, and Cornelia decided to withhold her paper's endorsement. Which meant our friendly lunch at Beachside Café would have to double as a strategy meeting because time was running out.

Chapter 15

Café Complications

THE SLIDER WAS HALFWAY to my mouth when I muttered to Merle, "This tastes like bribery."

The savory scent of grilled sirloin, cremini mushrooms, and caramelized onions floated in the air as the afternoon crowd buzzed inside the Beachside Café. Glen Phan, in his usual chef's whites despite not having set foot behind a grill in years, was working the room like a man possessed by ambition and marketing opportunities.

Pinned to his chest like a merit badge was a sparkling new *Vote Glen Phan* button. He handed out his steak and mushroom sliders with the same gusto he used to reserve for VIP diners, and people were eating it up. Literally.

Merle smirked. "You have to hand it to him. If the way to a voter's heart is through the stomach, Chef Glen is a shoo-in."

The man must have heard us talking about him because he made his way over, holding a tray like a magician about to reveal a trick.

"Boo!" he boomed, with good humor shining in his eyes. "May I interest you in another?"

He slid a warm little slider onto a napkin and handed it to me with a wink, then turned to Merle. "And thank you for keeping things friendly on the campaign trail, my friend. But then, it's not like either of us stands a chance next to Dodge. Am I right?"

His jovial laughter sounded sincere. So did Merle's, though my guy's eyes didn't quite agree with his mouth.

As Chef Glen moved on, I leaned across the table and whispered, "He doesn't know what he's talking about."

Merle smiled faintly, then looked down at the menu without really reading it.

We'd taken one of the last tables on the patio—which was really just a narrow strip of bistro tables corralled behind a black railing decorated with flower boxes bursting with cheerful pansies. A cool breeze was coming in off the shore, but I preferred it to being inside. Fewer eavesdroppers and a better view of the clear blue sky.

As we settled in, the aroma of rosemary and garlic drifted from the kitchen, which mingled with the sweet hibiscus in my iced tea. The floral notes were sharp at first sip, then mellowed into something unexpectedly soothing. Across from me, Merle studied the specials board.

"Jalapeño and Swiss burger," he decided.

I played it safe with a grilled chicken, bacon, and avocado sandwich. When Chef Glen came back to take our order, he raised a brow when I added a slice of vegan cheesecake to go.

"It's for Del," I added quickly.

He looked a little relieved. "She's still doing that vegan thing, huh? How's it going for her?"

"Oh, it's going," I said vaguely.

Which was true. It was going. Right into the garbage disposal when she wasn't looking—at least when she tried to serve that stuff to me.

Once Chef Glen headed back toward the kitchen—or more likely to glad-hand someone near the register—Merle leaned across the table. "I'm starting to think he's right. Neither of us stands much of a chance."

I glanced at him over my rosy red iced tea. "No way. Everybody has a chance. You especially. People know you, and they like you. That's a lot more than you can say about Tom Dodge. No one even elected him, if you'll remember. He's only on the council because Mallory appointed him to finish Aguirre's term."

Roland Aguirre had served on Laguna Bay's council for decades before a car accident left him nearly paralyzed. He'd moved up north to live with his son, who could care for him during his recovery. Mayor Mallory Haines hadn't wasted any time appointing her buddy Tom Dodge to fill the seat. Mallory, Tom, Eleanor, and even Cornelia Sloane all seemed to be cut from the same snooty cloth.

If Tom won, I had no doubt he'd appoint someone just as pro-business and development-happy as he was. Maybe that's why Eleanor Voss was cozying up to him. Or Cornelia, for that matter. I pulled my Hocus Focus notebook from my purse and jotted down both names.

"What's that?" Merle asked, eyeing my scribbles.

"Just keeping track of a few things," I said, flipping to a clean page.

"You know you can do that on your phone now, right?" He pulled his from his pocket and set it on the table. With a quick tap on the notepad icon, the screen shifted to a digital page that looked just like a real writing pad. "You can also record messages." He tapped another icon, and a digital recorder appeared on the screen. "The thing will even transcribe voice memos for easy reference. Comes in handy when you get an idea in the car."

"Nice," I said. "I'll have to remember that." Merle loved his gadgets, but I still trusted ink and paper. "Should we discuss questions Cornelia will probably ask during your interview?"

He shrugged as he dropped his phone back into his pocket. "Don't worry about that. I have it covered."

So much for our strategy session. I closed the notebook and pushed it aside.

When the silence stretched a little too long, Merle finally said, "How was your day?"

Who knew four little words could carry so much weight? I considered telling him about Fiona's ghost tearing through my shop, but I knew how Merle got when he thought I needed backup. He'd already rewired my entire fuse box and fixed the leaky washroom pipes.

Instead, I gave him the edited version.

"I had an interesting run-in with Councilman Dodge at the *Gazette* today. Am I crazy, or is there something not quite right about that guy?"

Merle raised an eyebrow. "Is that an either-or question? Because..." Then he cracked a smile. "Just kidding. Yeah. He seems a little too eager to be mayor. Or maybe my radar is off because I want the job too."

"I don't think your radar is off," I said as I smoothed the creases in my napkin and worked up the courage to ask my next question. "Did he have anything to do with the Channel Hotel before the fire?"

Merle didn't hesitate. "Nah. He wasn't even around then. His parents moved here in the 1970s after all the development in Anaheim swallowed their farm. Remember that? He used to visit, but he didn't live here full time until he inherited their place. That was, what? The nineties, I think."

I nodded slowly. I had a vague memory of that. Still, there was something about the way Tom operated that made my skin crawl. I almost reached for my notebook to jot down a reminder to dig into his real estate ties, but thought better of it. A mental note would have to do. No need to tip off Merle.

Then, I made another mental note: Stop thinking about the case. You're supposed to be enjoying a nice meal with Merle. Remember normal? Normal is good.

I changed the subject. "Are you sure you don't want to iron out your campaign strategy before you sit down with Cornelia?"

He hesitated. Not a long pause, but long enough to notice. "I'm still working it out," he said.

Which, coming from Merle, meant he was overthinking it. I wanted to tell him to trust his gut—that the town already liked him. But I also knew a person sometimes had to come to certain truths on their own.

Luckily, our food arrived, saving us both from having to dig deeper.

"I'll be right back." Merle slid back his chair. "Need to wash my hands."

I watched him go, then turned my attention back to my plate. The chicken was perfectly seared, the bacon crisp with just the right snap, and the avocado slices fanned out like flower petals. I took a small bite—smoky flavors giving way to a savory richness—and let myself sink into the gentle rhythm of clinking silverware and the low hum of conversation around me.

That's when I saw them.

Eleanor Voss and Tom Dodge, walking along the sidewalk from the boardwalk toward the café.

I ducked down and shielded my face with my hand, pretending to be engrossed in my plate and hoping my electric blue hair didn't give me away.

Their voices carried just enough over the restaurant's din. When Eleanor laughed, I peeked around the fingers resting on my cheek and saw her reaching out to touch Tom's arm. It lingered there.

Interesting.

Tom glanced around—furtive, like a man about to jaywalk in front of a police officer—and slipped something from his breast pocket into Eleanor's hand. It looked like an envelope.

She blinked with surprise. Her body stiffened, only slightly, but enough to notice. Was that confusion or fear?

He leaned in and whispered something in her ear. I didn't know what he said, but I recognized that kind of whisper. Quiet. Close. Controlling.

Her smile strained, then she shoved his envelope into her purse and scanned the area—nervous now. He smiled, smug and satisfied, and patted her shoulder.

Something about the whole thing left a sour taste in my mouth.

Eleanor had always struck me as proud. Polished. Not the kind of woman who flirted in public—especially not with a man like Tom Dodge—unless she had something to gain. But whatever had transpired between them, he seemed to have the upper hand.

Merle returned just as they disappeared around the corner.

He dropped back into his chair and caught the look on my face.

"Something wrong with the food?" he asked.

I set down my fork. "Eleanor Voss and Councilman Dodge just walked by, and I saw him hand her an envelope. Whatever was inside seemed to knock the wind out of her."

Merle raised an eyebrow. "Maybe it was a love note."

"Or a threat," I said quietly.

He leaned back. "That seems unlikely."

"Does it?" I asked. "I know what I saw."

He took a slow sip from his water glass. "Don't jump to conclusions."

It was a wise warning. But I wasn't jumping. I was edging toward a reasonable conclusion. If Councilman Dodge was cozying up to Eleanor, it was for more than professional reasons. I could feel it in my bones.

Chapter 16

The Séance

By the time Merle's porch light faded from my rearview mirror, a half-smile lingered on my face, one I hadn't worn in a long time. Our parting kiss, more suggestion than seduction, tasted faintly of vanilla. It wasn't explosive or cinematic, but it was sweet. Steady.

Of course, the moment I let myself feel anything resembling optimism, the universe usually threw a wrench wrapped in barbed wire through my front window. So, I was playing it cool. Still, as I pulled up outside the Boo-tique, I lingered in the memory of that warmth.

At least until I noticed the dark figure standing near the shop door. I braced as I shifted into park.

Either the streetlights were getting dimmer or my nighttime vision was getting worse because I couldn't quite make out whether that black silhouette was human, a supernatural, or a ghost. My stomach flipped. Was it Fiona?

Then the figure moved, and I saw the familiar bulky knitting bag.

"Willa," I muttered with relief. I called to her as I climbed out of the car. "You're early."

"I haven't done one of these in a while," she said, adjusting her shawl and the bag in her hand. "I may need some time to brush up. Also—" She paused, her tone shifting to that conspiratorial one she used for gossip—"I thought that reporter looked familiar, and now I know why."

I slowed my roll. "Fiona?"

She nodded. "When I was walking Pickles this afternoon, I ran into a neighbor from across the street. The woman was rattling on about how her tenant had died—wasn't sure if it was a car accident or a work thing. But she told me the young woman worked for the *Gazette*. It had to be Fiona. I must've seen her around the neighborhood."

Finally, a clue. Or at least a possible clue. "Did your neighbor mention any roommates? Friends? Anyone who might know what Fiona was working on?"

"She didn't. But I can ask." Willa's voice had a quiet determination to it. "I'll poke around a bit."

"Thanks," I said and meant it. "That could be a big help."

She nodded, but her attention had already drifted back to the shop. "Will Merle be joining us?"

I unlocked the door, buying myself a moment. "He's so busy with election stuff. I didn't want to bother him."

"Hmm," Willa replied, a sound that landed somewhere between doubt and judgment. "You know he'd drop everything if you needed him."

"I know." And I did. But even after the pleasant evening we'd had and that kiss, it just didn't feel right. Not yet. I guess I still needed more time.

Willa didn't answer as we stepped inside. She didn't have to.

I reached for the light switch and braced myself. I'd left the place in a mild state of chaos, sure, but my new resident ghost apparently had decided that wasn't dramatic enough.

Shelves were shifted. Candles knocked over. And the half-dozen cinnamon brooms I'd tucked neatly against the wall now formed a crooked trail down the center aisle.

"Oh, come on!" I groaned, kicking one aside. It spun, hit the end of a display of glittery plastic skulls, and sent one of them rolling toward me like a bowling ball.

Willa let out a low whistle. "She's definitely trying to get your attention."

"I wish she'd do it without destroying my shop," I grumbled.

The bell over the door jingled. Delphine, Jemma, and Opal breezed in, arms loaded with bags bearing Jemma's gelato shop logo. Kheppy followed behind them, tail up, chin lifted, and looking more alert than I'd seen her all week.

"Well, look who's up and about for a change," I said, crouching to scratch behind her ears.

"I'm feeling much better," Kheppy replied, her voice bright and chipper. "Just needed a bit of rest."

Delphine made a beeline for the front counter and started unloading small cups of icy confections. "We brought
refreshments."

"I can see that," I said and lit the shop candle to bring
some semblance of calm back to the place. "I thought
we were here to work, not drown our sorrows in frozen
desserts. My shop is under attack, in case no one noticed."
I gestured wildly at the wreckage around us.

Del held out a cup with a sheepish smile. "I brought you
pumpkin spice. You love pumpkin spice."

I glared at the offering. Technically, my sister should
have avoided the stuff. Gelato was just fancy ice cream as
far as I was concerned, and therefore should have been off
limits for a vegan.

Then again, I shouldn't be eating the stuff, either. My
doctor had told me if I didn't cut out sugar, or at least
cut back, she'd have to up the dosage of my blood pressure
pills. But I didn't care. Not tonight, anyway. I snatched the
cup and peeled off the lid. "Fine." I took a bite. "But let's
just remember why we're here."

Of course, it was ridiculously good.

Pumpkin, cinnamon, and a hint of something nut-
ty—like everything good about fall, condensed into one
magical confection. My shoulders dropped half an inch.

"Del," I said, mouth full, "thank you for this. It's delicious. And thank you, Jemma."

Once everyone had finished their treats, we got to work
clearing space for the séance. Brooms were stashed, toppled decorations set upright, and I even found a box of

127

thick candles Willa declared perfect for the ritual. As the five of us moved through the shop, tidying and arranging, Kheppy prowled the perimeter—her nose twitching, movements just a touch more alert than usual. "Do you sense her?" I inquired.

Kheppy paused, tail swaying. "Something is here. Or was. But it's different."

Great. Just what I needed—vague spectral vibes and a few open flames. I surveyed the candles and frowned. "Does anyone remember where I keep my fire extinguisher?"

No one answered. Not a great sign.

Willa cleared her throat. "Ready to get started, ladies? Take your places."

Opal grabbed one of my hands, Delphine took the other. Jemma took a spot, and Willa stepped in to close the circle. She glanced up at Kheppy, who had perched atop a bookcase to watch.

"Would you like to join?" Willa asked our feline friend. "You're more than welcome."

"I will observe, thank you," Kheppy said.

Willa nodded, closed her eyes, and began softly invoking the elements, her whispered words flowing like water over stone.

"Spirit of fire, spirit of air, spirit of water, and spirit of earth. Guardians of this space, we ask for your protection. Fiona, if you are here, we invite you. We want to help you. Show us a sign, if you're able."

All around, candle flames flickered.

The one sitting in the center of the circle snuffed itself out with a soft hiss.

Jemma scrambled forward to relight it. As she returned to her spot and joined hands again, a sudden draft tore through the shop, extinguishing every one of our candles.

"Really?" I muttered.

The room plunged into inky darkness. Just as I reached for my phone's flashlight, a voice echoed—low, feminine, and unfamiliar.

"Can you hear me?" the voice said.

It was distorted, as though it came from the bottom of a well.

"Can anyone hear me?"

My heart leaped. "Fiona?"

A tiny click, and one candle in the center of the circle flickered back to life, revealing Kheppy standing there beside it.

"This isn't the time for your impersonations, Kheppy," I scolded. But as I tried to shoo her away, I noticed the dull, blank expression in her eyes.

Her fur stood on end, fluffing her tail to twice its normal size. Whatever this was, it wasn't her usual shenanigans. Kheppy hardly seemed to be in control of anything at all. I'd never seen her like this.

Her mouth opened, and Fiona's voice emerged. "Hurry." Again, the voice sounded strangely distant. "They're searching. You must stop them."

"Stop who?" I asked frantically. "What are we supposed to—?"

"Shh!" Willa hissed. "Fiona, we hear you," she said more calmly. "Can you tell us more? Can you show us?"

Kheppy's eyes glazed. Her head lolled to the side.

Then her body stiffened.

"Save the files."

The words struck like an electric shock. A heartbeat later, another gust blew through the room—wild and ice cold—and extinguished the solitary flame. Just before the light went out, I saw Kheppy collapse.

I rushed to her side and scooped her gently into my arms. My heart pounded with fear.

"I am all right," she murmured, dazed but conscious. "Just... need... a moment."

Her fur was cold against my skin, and her heartbeat fluttered like a trapped moth.

The others whispered among themselves as they relit the candles.

"Files," I repeated aloud. "Did she mean city hall files? Or the *Gazette*? Or—"

Another gust swept through the shop and through me. It filled me, and I could see them. Folders neatly stacked on a small wooden table. Then the image vanished, leaving me woozy.

I handed Kheppy to Delphine. "Get her some water. Or something to eat, if she wants it. Anything. Willa, will you come with me?"

Delphine stared at me, confused—they all did—as I grabbed my purse and keys and headed for the front door. Willa followed.

"Where are you going?" my sister asked.

I was already out the door. Over my shoulder, I called back to her, "To Fiona's place. The answers are there. I know it. And if someone is after them, I have to get there first."

"But you can't just break in!" Del bellowed.

I glanced back. "Oh, yeah? Watch me."

In Delphine's arms, I swear I saw Kheppy's lips stretch into a grin. Then she shook her head, and said, "That's my human."

Chapter 17

Broken Window

THE TIRES OF MY Karmann Ghia hummed over the cracked pavement along Laguna Bay's side streets. Headlights cut a narrow beam through the mist, throwing shadows against the squat beach bungalows that lined the road like sleepy sentinels. The salt air clung to my skin, sticky and cool, as the adrenaline from the séance coursed through my veins.

Willa sat in the passenger seat, clutching her knitting bag and sending occasional glances my way.

"I appreciate the ride home, Boo," she said, her voice soft yet anxious. "But what did you mean when you said you were going to break into that woman's place?" She sat back and adjusted her glasses. "You can't be serious."

"I'm dead serious," I said. "If Fiona was working on a story that got her killed, she must have gotten her hands on something big. She didn't keep files at the *Gazette*, so she must have kept them at home."

"Then why not turn that information over to the police and let them investigate?"

My friend was right to ask. Turning over important information related to a murder investigation would ordinarily be the right thing to do. But this was not an ordinary murder investigation. I'd been going over the arguments, and I couldn't see any way around it.

"That detective already thinks I've lost my marbles," I muttered, flicking on the turn signal as we approached her street. "He won't take me seriously."

"Do you know that for a fact?" she pressed.

I hesitated, then lied through my teeth. "Yes. I do."

Maybe he hadn't said it in so many words, but I could feel the skepticism in his voice every time I opened my mouth. If I started talking about séances and ghostly warnings, he'd probably have me committed.

"If I tell him about the files, I'll have to explain how I know about them. That means the ghost and the séance. How do you think that conversation will go?" I glanced at her. "The less he knows about anything that can be linked to our supernatural community, the better."

Willa opened her mouth to argue, then shut it again and shook her head. "You may have a point."

I turned onto Willa's street—a charming ribbon of road barely wide enough for two cars to pass. Most of the homes were vintage cottages from the 1920s and 1930s, painted in cheerful pastels. Some had been subdivided into tiny duplexes, hardly big enough to hold a sofa and a bed, while others had been lavishly enlarged far beyond their original glory.

Willa pointed to a powder-blue house, low and modest, with a pair of stubby sago palms in the yard and drapes pulled tightly across a wide front window.

"That's the one," Willa said. "Fiona's place is in the back. The entrance is around the side."

I pulled into my friend's driveway, admiring her tidy yellow home with wind chimes clinking faintly in the breeze. She gathered her bag and slid out.

"Just give me a minute to put my things inside," she said.

I got out of the car as she shuffled to her front door, fumbled with her keys, and tucked the bag inside without going in. She shut the door and returned to the car. "Okay. What's the plan?"

I buttoned up my denim jacket to fight off the cold. "What do you mean?"

"Are we going over now? Or do you want to stake out the place first?"

It took me a second to process what she was proposing. "We're not doing anything. You can't come."

Even in the dim amber glow from the nearby streetlights, I could see her glaring at me. "Excuse me?"

"I mean, it's better if you don't. If I get caught, there's no point in both of us going to jail."

Willa stiffened, insulted. "I'm not afraid of jail."

"No one said you were. I just..." I rubbed my forehead, feeling the start of a stress headache blooming behind my left eyebrow. "Look, if you could keep an eye out and text me if someone comes around—especially the police—then maybe no one will be going to jail."

She hesitated, clearly weighing whether to accept this compromise. Then she offered a single, crisp nod. "Fine. I'll stay here and be your lookout."

"Thank you," I exhaled. "But maybe hang back by the side of your house, in the shadows. Keep your phone ready to message me if you see something."

Willa pulled out her device and frowned at it. "Maybe you could show me where that text thing is again."

I groaned. "Just call me. That'll be easier. If you see anyone—anyone at all—call."

We parted with a nod, and I crept across the street, each step making my heart thump a little louder. A low mist wrapped around my ankles like ghostly fingers—which made me regret every horror movie I'd ever seen.

The powder-blue house was quiet. I followed the narrow path around to the back and found the door—white trim with mullioned windows and a white curtain covering the inside for privacy.

I twisted the knob.

Locked.

Of course it was locked. How could I possibly think this would be easy?

I lifted the doormat, then tipped the potted gardenias, searching all the usual places people stored spare keys. Nothing. Scanning the side of the house, I spotted a window, but it was too high off the ground to reach. Another one farther away was too narrow to squeeze through. I pressed my hand to the door's glass, peering between the curtain and the door frame, to see what was inside.

Bookcase. Couch. A coffee table covered in—

My pulse stuttered. Those weren't magazines. They were folders. A whole stack of them.

Fiona's files. Just like my vision.

"Okay," I muttered. "We're doing this."

I pulled off my jacket, wrapped the denim around my hand, and punched the small pane closest to the lock.

It hurt.

A lot.

What was more irritating, the glass didn't even crack.

I cursed under my breath, took a step back, and punched again, throwing every ounce of frustration, grief, and rage I had at that pane.

The window shattered, scattering glass on the floor inside and around my feet.

I waited, holding my breath and listening in case the commotion had alerted someone to come investigate.

Nothing.

Heart racing, I widened the hole so I could reach through and unlock the door. Then I slipped inside, stepping cautiously around the shards.

The scent of citrus air freshener greeted me in the darkness. I closed the door behind me and locked it.

When I turned back to the table, my phone buzzed in my pocket. I fumbled it out, expecting a warning from Willa.

Nope.

Just a cheerful reminder from my health provider that my blood pressure medication was due for a refill and would I like to order it now?

I swiped the screen to dismiss the message and muttered something unladylike. As the screen went dark, it occurred to me to use the phone's flashlight function. Not as good as a proper one, but better than nothing.

I found the icon and turned the stream of light on the coffee table.

Among the files were notes, invoices, and newspaper clippings—names circled in red ink. "Channel Hotel" had been scrawled across more than one manila folder, along with the words "Blackmail" and "Lies." I sat down to sift through the pile, my hands trembling.

Crunch.

The sound froze me in place.

Crunch.

Someone—or something—was stepping on the shards on the other side of the door.

I checked my phone.

Nothing from Willa.

In the silvery moonlight, I could see a silhouette behind the curtain. The doorknob clicked as it tried to turn.

Panic surged through me. I grabbed everything I could get my hands on and hugged it to my chest like a life raft. My brain flipped through hiding places—behind the couch? In a closet? Could I make it to the kitchen and slip out the side window?

Too late.

A dark, gloved hand reached through the broken window and around the curtain to twist the bolt.

As the door creaked open, my body acted before my brain did.

I ran.

Straight toward the door.

Straight at the intruder.

I barreled over the threshold, knocking the darkly dressed figure off balance. The intruder grunted—a sound of surprise and pain. I didn't stop to look, but as I shoved by, a sickly sweet scent hit me. Not what I would expect from a burglar, but what did I know about criminal behavior?

"Run, Boo," I whispered to myself. "Just run."

And that's exactly what I did.

Chapter 18

Buried Past

THE MOMENT I STEPPED into the kitchen, the kettle on the stove let out a shrill whistle like it had just seen a ghost. Fitting, really, considering the night I'd had.

The night we'd *all* had.

Delphine, wearing her green terry robe and a scowl, pulled the water off the burner. Two long gray braids hung over her shoulders like ropes.

"I think the light in my room might still be off," she said, one eyebrow arched.

"Very funny," I muttered, reaching around to flip on a living room lamp I'd missed on my first pass through the house. "Next time you break into a dead woman's place and come face-to-face with a burglar, you can lecture me on energy efficiency."

"So, now it was a burglar?" she asked, setting the kettle down with a clink. "A few minutes ago, it was an intruder. What if it was the landlady? She may have heard you breaking in and wanted to investigate."

"It wasn't the landlady." I tried to sound confident.

Truth was, it could have been anyone, including the landlady. All I'd seen was a dark figure wearing a black ski mask. That wasn't something a kindly octogenarian would wear if she were checking on her rental after midnight. When I'd stumbled into Willa's place after making my getaway, panting and wide-eyed, she'd agreed with me.

Still, that didn't stop Del from drilling me like I was the suspect.

"You really have no idea who it was?" she pressed with a hefty dose of skepticism.

I slumped into a chair at the kitchen table, where I'd spread out Fiona's files. "No clue. I told you. It was too dark, and their face was covered."

"But you must have noticed something. Was it a man or a woman? Tall? Short? A mustache? Just think for a second. It might come to you."

She was trying to help. Her voice was soft, encouraging even. But the last thing I wanted to do was replay the moment I'd nearly screamed my lungs out while running from someone who may or may not have intended to kill me. Or at least hurt me. I'd spent the last hour trying to shake off the terror clawing at my chest.

Kheppy, bless her immortal soul, seemed to understand.

Delphine said our furry friend had fallen asleep soon after I left them at the shop and had stayed that way as she drove them both home. Del had left Kheppy curled on my bed, where the cat remained until I came barreling through the front door with my arms full of Fiona's files. I'd dumped the haul on the kitchen table before making my way through the house, switching on every bulb I could find, illuminating every shadowy corner.

From outside, our place was probably brighter than an LAX runway—because I wasn't in the mood for any more surprises hiding in the dark.

When she heard me, Kheppy padded into the kitchen, tail swaying, and settled beside me like a tiny lioness on high alert. She studied me for a long moment, then jumped into my lap with the precision of an Olympic gymnast.

The second her warm weight settled against me and that comforting purr kicked in, the tightness in my chest finally loosened.

"How are you, sweetheart?" I whispered, scratching the soft spot behind her ears. "You surprised me tonight. I didn't know you could channel spirits."

Her tawny eyes met mine. "I didn't know, either. I did not like it."

I grinned, knowing the feeling all too well. "I'm sorry it happened that way."

"It was not your fault," she said. "That ghost was full and surprised."

I bit my lip so I wouldn't laugh. "Do you mean *full of surprises*?"

"Yes. That is what I meant."

There was something about her mangled phrases that always melted my heart. She was trying. Like me, in a way. Trying to hold it together, trying to make sense of a world spinning out of control.

Delphine returned with a tray: a pot of steaming lemon-chamomile tea, two mismatched mugs, and a plate of shortbread cookies that looked surprisingly buttery. Not a chia seed or kelp flake in sight.

"You made the real ones?" I asked, eyeing the treats with suspicion.

"You've had a rough night," she said. "I thought you would appreciate real butter."

"Don't let my doctor hear you say that," I said.

"Then it can be our secret." She poured the tea and sat beside me, her eyes scanning the mess of folders, clippings, and handwritten notes covering the table.

"So," she said, "what are we looking for?"

I took a long sip of the tea—enjoying the citrus and delicate floral notes—and tried to make sense of the chaos in front of me.

"These are Fiona's files," I said. "They were out, like she'd been going through them before..."

Before what? Before we found her in the alley? Before she was murdered? Before she became the ghost haunting my shop? I couldn't bring myself to say it. I stashed away that painful memory and trudged onward.

"This is what she was working on and what might have caused the trouble."

Delphine's brow creased. "You think something here might have gotten her killed?"

Another gut punch, but I managed to nod.

One by one, I opened the folders and flipped through their contents—mostly headlines, articles about the

Channel Hotel fire, old property records, and notes written in Fiona's neat, deliberate hand. From what I could piece together, she'd been tracking the site's ownership, which seemed to pass through a maze of shell companies. Across several photocopies, she'd scrawled the word blackmail? in bold strokes, but if she'd uncovered any solid proof, her notes didn't show it.

I searched in vain for a link to Councilman Tom Dodge—or to anyone, really. The evidence didn't point to a clear suspect, but one thing was certain: Fiona had been onto something. I just couldn't see what—yet.

"This wasn't just a fishing expedition," I said quietly. "She knew what she was looking for. There are letters from city officials, maintenance reports, complaints from residents. Somehow it all relates to that fire."

Delphine leaned closer, squinting at a creased clipping. A black-and-white photo of a blonde woman on the Channel Hotel porch stared back at us. Big hair, big smile, and a silky dress with the biggest shoulders I'd ever seen.

"Maureen Calvert?"

I nodded. "She shows up a lot. That woman sure loved shoulder pads."

"You have to admit, they looked good on her," Del said wistfully.

I pulled out a thick folder marked Calvert. Inside were more clippings, typed reports, and near the back, a yellowed carbon copy of a social worker's form. I handed it to Del.

"Enrollment in foster care," she said, reading aloud. "Fifteen-year-old female. Name: Eloise Calvert. Mother: Maureen Calvert."

I'd nearly forgotten about Eloise, the daughter Maureen had left behind when she'd fled. I sighed and shook my head. "That poor girl."

"I'll never understand how a mother could abandon her child the way she did," Delphine said, her voice tight. "It breaks my heart."

Mine too.

I pulled the next page from the stack—a handwritten letter addressed to a foster parent, regarding placement logistics. I set it aside.

The letter beneath it stopped my breath.

It was from a foster mother, addressed to a social services administrator. She was asking how to emancipate Eloise—seventeen at the time—so the girl could marry her boyfriend. The request was marked urgent.

Urgent?

I flipped the page.

Behind it was a yellowed, slightly blurry snapshot of a courthouse wedding. The bride wore a tea-length dress and a bashful smile. The young man beside her looked like he'd borrowed a larger man's suit.

I turned it over.

Eloise and Jim Richards had been written on the back in black ink.

Something sharp twisted in my chest.

I rifled through the folder, suddenly frantic, until I found it—a birth certificate.

Fiona Maureen Richards.

Mother: Eloise Calvert Richards.

Father: James Richards.

I stared at that tattered slip, my breath stuck somewhere in my throat.

"Del," I whispered. "This is it."

She leaned in to read the document, her expression shifting from confusion to stunned recognition.

"But how—" she began. I lifted a hand to stop her.

"Fiona is Maureen Calvert's granddaughter," I whispered as a heaviness filled the room.

Fiona hadn't just been investigating the Channel Hotel fire—she was chasing her own family history. The woman who had caused this town so much pain was Fiona's flesh and blood.

My skin prickled with a chill that had nothing to do with the breeze slipping through the partly opened window.

"This is why Fiona won't move on," I murmured. "This is her unfinished business. It has to be."

Across the table, Kheppy lifted her head, ears twitching. "She must have wanted you to find this. She wants people to know the truth."

I rose from the table slowly, the pieces falling into place in my mind. Fiona had died trying to understand her family's buried past. And now that story had landed squarely in my lap.

Del glanced up, worried. "What are you going to do?"

145

In that moment, I knew there was only one thing I could do. "I have to go back to the shop," I said. "If Fiona's still there, it's time we had a real conversation."

Chapter 19
Seven of Cups

THE FLAME SPUTTERED AS I struck the match too hard, sending a fine spray of sulfur into the air. It burned my nose, sharp and acrid, but I leaned in anyway, lighting the last of the candles arranged in a loose circle on the floor of the Boo-tique. Midnight was long gone, and I had no business being awake, let alone trying to chat with a ghost by myself. But here we were.

From her perch on the counter, Kheppy watched me in silence, her amber eyes catching the candlelight and gleaming like twin shards of topaz in the dark.

"Spirit of the departed," I said, beginning slow and dramatic as Willa had done earlier that night. "We call upon you to join this circle. Reveal your truth... illuminate the shadows..."

Delphine, who had refused to stay home, cleared her throat softly.

"Shh!" I waved a hand at her without looking. "I'm trying to focus."

I closed my eyes more tightly and strained to remember the next part. Something about welcoming the spirit across the veil? Or was it opening a channel?

"We ask you to, uh... communicate through... the light of—" I stumbled, pushed back a few strands of electric blue hair, and opened my eyes. "Forget it. I don't have the patience for this."

I recalibrated and tried again.

"Fiona," I said plainly. "I know you're Maureen Calvert's granddaughter, and I know that had something to do with your story about the Channel Hotel. If you're hanging around here because you have unfinished business, you need to tell me what it is if you want my help. Whatever it is, I'm listening."

Silence.

Not even the creak of the shop walls settling. Just the steady burn of candlelight and the distant hum of the mini refrigerator in the back office.

Del shifted beside me and pushed up the sleeves of the red hoodie she'd pulled on over her pajamas as we rushed out the door. She'd been so dead-set against letting me come back to the shop alone that she hadn't even bothered to put on proper pants. As she hovered outside the circle of candles, her long gray braids swinging down her back, she started to sway—just a little. That usually meant one of three things: her foot had fallen asleep, her bunion was acting up, or she was about to share an opinion I hadn't asked for. When she crossed her arms and tapped her lip with one finger, I knew exactly which direction we were headed.

"Maybe she doesn't know how to respond," Del suggested. "Try something simpler. A yes or no question. Tell her to give us a sign if the answer is yes."

I gave my sister a look, but she shrugged and adjusted the collar of her hoodie. "It's worth a try."

Del always did that—tried to make the hard stuff simpler. I'd spent years teasing her for her fussiness, but honestly, I often leaned on her quiet insistence more than I cared to admit.

I addressed the empty air.

"Fiona," I repeated, but more slowly this time. "Are you Maureen Calvert's granddaughter? Is that why you were looking into the Channel Hotel fire? If the answer is yes... do something. Rattle a broom or fog up a window—I'm not picky."

Nothing.

I frowned and pressed my palms against my eyeballs. "It's a simple question. If she has something to say, I'm sure she could find a way to say it."

Del was already raising a finger. "Technically, you asked two questions."

Before I could snap back, Kheppy spoke up. "Boo?" she asked meekly.

"Not now," I groused, staring hard at my sister as I prepared to defend myself.

"Boo," she said again, more harshly.

I clenched my eyes shut and rolled my fingers into fists at my side. "May I finish my thought? Please?"

"Boo."

I finally spun to face my feline friend. "What?!"

Kheppy wasn't looking at me. She was staring past me to the corner shelf filled with tarot cards. Kheppy's sleek gray fur bristled down her back like she was riding an electric current.

My animal companion, who had once napped through an entire earthquake, now stood alert and unmoving. Elegant, unshakable, and ancient in ways I could only imagine, Kheppy had never been just a cat. She was a whiskered enigma with a voice as smooth as velvet and a stare that cut through lies like a hot blade through butter.

A shimmer hovered in the air near that corner shelf. The image wavered, then slowly coalesced into the outline of a woman. Young. Tall. Lips moving without sound, as though she were engaged in a silent conversation.

It took a moment to find my voice. "We can't hear you," I said. "Can you speak louder?"

The ghost's form flickered like an old black-and-white movie, mouth still moving.

Then—*thwack!*—several decks of tarot cards launched from the shelf beside her and landed at my feet, the boxes scattering in a circle.

Del made a soft sound in her throat. "Well. I'd say that message is pretty clear."

My stomach sank. "No."

Kheppy padded forward, her tail curled like a hook. "You can do this, Boo," she urged softly. "The cards spoke to you before. They might speak to you again."

"She's right, Boo," Del whispered.

I shook my head. They still thought I was afraid the cards wouldn't speak to me.

But that wasn't it.

Not even close.

I was afraid they'd speak as clearly and coldly as they had that day all those years ago, when I'd told a young woman what I'd seen of her future, and she had blamed me for every misfortune that followed. That reading had stuck with me for years. I'd carried it with me every time I reached for the deck. I'd told myself I was protecting people by giving up the cards. But really, I was protecting myself.

I'd stayed away from them for decades without looking back, but my sister had convinced me to seek the cards' help recently when I was trying to clear my name from an injustice. She was right. They had helped. But I wasn't sure I was ready to give them another chance.

My sister must have seen the struggle on my face. She moved closer and touched my arm. "I know it must be difficult, but don't give in to that stubborn streak of yours. The cards might help. You'll never know if you don't try."

I wanted to tell her she didn't know what she was talking about, but—as usual—she did. As much as I hated to admit it, Delphine was right.

I picked up one of the boxes and slid the deck into my hand. It was a traditional Rider–Waite Tarot deck, which had always been my favorite. I went to the counter and gave the cards a shaky shuffle. Old reflexes kicked in, and I almost offered the deck to Fiona to cut before catching myself.

Instead, I turned to Del. "Care to do the honors?"

She nodded solemnly, took the cards, split them into three neat piles, then reassembled them with the same quiet care she gave her herb bundles and seed trays.

I held the deck in my hands and took a deep breath. The possibilities for spreads swam through my thoughts—Celtic Cross, Three Fates, Fourfold Vision—but I shook them off. I didn't need a spread.

I had one question, so I only needed one card.

I lifted the top one and flipped it over.

Seven of Cups.

A silhouetted figure stared up at seven floating goblets, each filled with something strange and tempting—a snake, a laurel wreath, a ghostly face.

All the usual meanings flowed through me. Confusion. Wishful thinking. Illusion.

The one that stood out was confusion. Was the card telling me Fiona didn't know the answer? Or that she didn't know how to communicate it?

I showed the card to Del. Her brow wrinkled.

"Pull another one," she whispered. "For clarification."

The ghostly form shimmered, then fractured like a radio signal breaking up.

Kheppy's ears twitched. "She is losing energy. We don't have much time." She hesitated. "Tell her she may possess me again if it would help."

That stopped me.

This cat—my friend, my best friend—was willing to do that again after the toll it had taken?

Kheppy wasn't just brave. She was loyal in a way I wasn't sure I deserved.

"You'd let her do that?" I asked, my voice straining.

Her nose wrinkled. "I am not happy about it. But I will. It may help."

That small, powerful voice of hers—so calm, so composed—held more courage and conviction than most people managed in a lifetime.

I scratched the top of her head. "Thank you, darling," I said. "But no."

She blinked up at me. "Are you sure?"

"I am. I do need help, but not from you. Not this time."

I looked at the broken circle of candles and the cards still clutched in my hand. My gaze drifted toward my purse, sitting beside the register with my phone peeking from the front pocket.

This whole night—this whole investigation—had been me trying to prove I could do it alone. That I didn't need to call in favors or rely on anyone. Especially not Merle.

But that ghost wasn't talking, and I was out of ideas.

I grabbed my phone and stared at the contact list.

Merle Foster.

My thumb hovered over his name, the screen cold beneath my skin. I didn't want to call him. Didn't want to need him. But I did.

If anyone knew how to talk to a stubborn ghost—or a stubborn woman—it was Merle.

I hit the call button and held my breath, hoping he'd pick up.

Chapter 20

Ghostly Assistance

BY THE TIME MERLE knocked on the shop door, I was equal parts hopeful and nauseous.

He stepped inside the Boo-tique, smelling of salt air and coffee, his boots thudding softly against the floor. His flannel shirt hung askew, like he'd thrown it on in a hurry.

"What happened here?" he asked, looking around at the mess Fiona had, once again, inflicted on my shop. "When you said emergency, I thought you meant plumbing or wiring. Is everyone all right? Were you here when the burglars broke in?"

I could see how he'd jumped to that conclusion, considering the mess, and I wasn't looking forward to setting him straight. But like it or not, that's what I had to do. I looked at the candle wax dribbled on the floor and the piles of broken décor. "The place wasn't robbed," I said. "It's haunted."

Merle's brows knit together. "Come again?"

"Fiona's here," I admitted, barely above a whisper.

My sister must have sensed I was losing my nerve because she jumped in. "She wrecks the place, Boo tidies it, then she tears it up again."

Merle turned to me slowly. "How long has this been going on?"

I shifted, the unease clawing at my chest. "It started when the detective took you in for questioning."

His silence stretched, heavier than any words. We'd talked since then—more than once, and for hours. Every conversation had been an opportunity to come clean. And I hadn't taken any of them.

"Why didn't you tell me?" he asked quietly, the hurt plain in his voice.

Why didn't I? I'd asked myself that same question half a dozen times already. Part of it was to protect him while he focused on the election. Part of it was my pride, maybe. Another part was fear.

"I didn't want to burden you," I said finally. "You've got the campaign—and everything else—to deal with."

He nodded, but his eyes said he knew that wasn't the full story. And he was right. Deep down, I didn't know if I could trust him. He'd behaved so strangely with Fiona—and then that incident in his backyard with the files? I didn't want to suspect him of something terrible, but I was having a hard time reconciling what he'd told me with what I'd seen with my own eyes.

I wasn't sure I trusted him, and I definitely wasn't sure I could trust myself to think clearly when it came to him.

When I saw that realization flash in his eyes, it stung more than I expected.

"I was trying to protect you," I added. I was only digging a deeper hole, so I stopped.

He took a breath and squared his shoulders. "Where has the activity been strongest?"

"Here at the front of the shop," I said, gesturing at the disarray.

Merle sighed. "She came in that day. The day she died." His mouth pressed into a line, and I knew he was remembering it, the way she'd confronted him, all hot and full of fire. He didn't say anything. Just sighed again.

"We held a séance with Willa, Opal, and Jemma," I added. "I even tried the tarot. We got a few words out of her, but not enough to find out why she's here. She must have some unfinished business, right?"

He shrugged those big shoulders of his, but he still wouldn't meet my gaze. "That's usually the case." He rubbed his chin and walked slowly through the aisles, stopping to examine the shattered ceramic bats and the toppled display of plastic pumpkins.

When he came back to the center, that hurt expression was gone. "All right," he said. "You, Del, and Kheppy should stay back. If she's still here and she gets upset, I don't want anyone getting hurt."

I gathered Kheppy in my arms and led Del to the corridor behind the cash register. We squeezed into the doorway and watched Merle push the candles to the edge of the room. He moved to the center and spoke to the ceiling like it might talk back.

"Fiona?" he said. "You're not alone. We want to help."

"Do you see her?" I asked. "Is she here?"

Merle glanced over his shoulder and grimaced. "Quiet, please."

I zipped my lips and mimed tossing the key into a mini black cauldron on the shelf beside me.

He closed his eyes and continued to coax the reluctant ghost to reveal herself. His words filled the room in a low, rhythmic tone. The candles guttered. The air thickened. And then...

Boom.

A wall of ghostly wind swept through the shop. A ceramic skull soared past, taking out a brass candelabra filled with battery-powered tapers. Bats boomeranged through the air, colliding mid-flight. One hit the register with a sad clunk.

"She's mad," Del muttered, ducking.

"No kidding," I hissed.

Kheppy wriggled out of my arms and dove under the counter. Smart girl.

Merle's voice rose above the melee. "Fiona. We're trying to understand. Help us."

Another crash. This time a garland of miniature witch hats went sailing through the air like festive shrapnel.

Merle staggered back. Sweat beaded on his temples. He shook his head.

"She won't talk to me," he said. "She's here, but she's not listening."

"So, what do we do?" I asked. "She's going to put me out of business, or worse, hurt someone."

He hesitated.

"There is someone who might be able to reach her," he said. "But you're not going to like it."

I folded my arms. "I'm way past the point of liking any of this. I just want it to stop. Who do you have in mind?"

"Rupert."

My stomach sank.

Del sucked in a breath and answered for me. "That shouldn't be a problem. That's all ancient history, right, Boo? Forgive and forget?"

Ancient, yes. Forgiven? Nope. Forgotten? Absolutely not.

Rupert had been the final straw back when Merle and I were young and foolish and maybe halfway to the altar. He might have been a ghost, even back then, but he'd also been a solid wall between Merle and me. Always whispering into Merle's ear. I couldn't compete with a smug, spectral companion who never slept and had opinions about everything.

I'd packed my bags the same week Rupert started offering unsolicited advice about my cooking skills—or lack thereof.

But tonight wasn't about old wounds.

It was about answers.

"Fine," I said. "Call him."

"He's already here," Merle said.

The room went still. The candles flared.

Then he appeared—tall, faintly glowing, and as insufferably composed as ever.

The second Rupert manifested, the temperature dropped fifteen degrees. As the rest of us shivered, his form flickered like a computer screen on the fritz. "Good evening, Boo," he said, his voice as smooth as over-polished silverware.

"Let's skip the pleasantries, please?" I said.

"Of course," he replied.

Merle ignored us both. He looked up again. "Fiona, what are you trying to tell us?"

A shimmer pulsed in the air behind Rupert, like heat rising off asphalt. At first, it was just a ripple—barely there, easy to dismiss. But then it thickened into shape, and for a split second, we saw her.

Fiona.

She stood behind Rupert, faint as moonlight, her features soft and sorrowful. Her long hair drifted as though floating underwater, framing a face that appeared worn but resolute. Her eyes—translucent but unmistakably hers—were wide and haunted as she gazed at us from across that mortal divide.

She wore the same clothes she'd had on the last time I saw her: that large blazer and skinny jeans. But now the colors were leached, the edges blurred like a watercolor left out in the rain. She wasn't whole. Not really. But she was there.

Her ghostly hand rose slowly, fingers trembling as they reached for Rupert's shoulder. She didn't touch him, not quite. Just hovered—then she stepped forward with hesitant grace.

As her form passed into Rupert, he jerked like a marionette yanked into position. His chest seized. His hands clenched. And then he gasped, loud and startled.

The candles flared, their flames reaching high for a beat before returning to normal.

The overlapping forms shimmered more brightly, blurring together until it was impossible to say where Rupert ended and Fiona began. Then their overlapped hands twitched and shot forward. Their mouths opened and closed twice before words emerged. It was Fiona's voice—coarse and tired, like it had traveled a long way to get here.

"The truth... buried... buried deep..."

Then silence.

The candles flared again, and the forms split apart. Rupert staggered back, one hand bracing against the nearest shelf, ghostly fingers passing through the wood. Fiona's form drifted to the side before melting into the ether.

"She's fading," Rupert said, his deep tenor sounding winded. "But that was her message to you. It cost her dearly."

Del clutched my arm. "But what does it mean? What's buried? Is she talking about the cemetery?"

Kheppy had left her hiding place to perch beside the register. "She said truth. Could she mean a truth buried in her files?"

I thought Kheppy was onto something, but that word, buried, made me think of something else.

"I think she's talking about Cornelia," I said, the certainty settling in even as I spoke.

They all turned toward me, even Rupert.

"Cornelia protects our supernatural community by controlling what makes it onto the newspaper's pages, by burying stories that reveal too much. Maybe Fiona was looking for something she never found because Cornelia had buried it. It would explain why she hadn't kept her files at the office."

It was the only explanation that made sense.

Chapter 21

Red Velvet

THE BENCH IN FRONT of the *Laguna Bay Gazette* had seen better days—and so had I. My right hip ached, my electric blue hair was a frizzy mess, and the coastal damp had wormed its way through my denim jacket and sunk deep into my bones. I'd given myself plenty of time to vote at the library—maybe too much. I'd strolled in, slipped behind the curtain, cast my ballot, and walked right back out.

It was barely past eight, and I'd already been parked on this splinter-happy bench long enough to lose feeling in my backside.

I cupped my cold hands around a lukewarm travel mug of green tea—courtesy of Delphine—and stared at the *Gazette*'s locked glass door like sheer stubbornness could will Cornelia Sloane into materializing.

My phone buzzed in my jacket pocket just as I was building up a solid, silent rant. I dug it out and saw Sissy's name glowing on the screen.

Dread flooded through me. I'd forgotten all about her. Even worse, I'd forgotten to tell her I was keeping the shop closed for another day.

I tapped the answer button. "Sissy! Please tell me you're not at the shop already." She wasn't. Thank goodness. "I won't be opening today. So, you get another paid day off." I tried to sound upbeat, like it was a well-earned reward instead of the result of my continued failure to rid the place of a cranky ghost.

There was a pause. "Oh, uh... okay," she said hesitantly. "The leak still hasn't been fixed?"

I frowned. "The what?"

Another pause.

Oh. Right. That had been yesterday's excuse.

I cleared my throat. "Sorry, I thought you said heat. I've got the phone on my bad ear."

Sissy giggled, though she was being generous. "No worries. Honestly, I was calling to let you know I might be late. My mom and I stopped to vote, and there's a pretty long line."

"Now you can take all the time you need," I said, trying to sound like the election was the single-most important thing on my mind. Which it should have been, but sadly wasn't. "And, in case I haven't said it enough, Merle and I appreciate your support."

"You must be swamped with last-minute campaign stuff," she said. "Do you need help with anything?"

For a second, my heart pinched. Sissy wasn't just a good employee, she was a good human. Loyal, eager, and sweet as pumpkin pie. "That's real nice of you, honey. But we've got it covered."

"Okay," she said. "Let me know if that changes. Otherwise, I'll see you at Merle's election party. What time is it starting?"

Oh, brother. The party—like everything else—had completely slipped my mind. "Can you do me a favor and check with Merle on that? We've moved the party to his place, and I'm not sure about the time. Actually, if you could help spread the word about the change, it would really help." I winced, sure that would set off her alarm bells that something unusual was up.

But, nope. She said, "Yeah, no problem," still chipper as could be.

As soon as we hung up, I texted Merle to tell him about the new party location and to beg forgiveness for dumping it in his lap at the last minute.

I'd barely hit the send button when a sleek black sedan nosed into a reserved spot in the *Gazette* parking lot like it belonged there—because apparently it did.

Cornelia Sloane stepped out, pristine as ever in a pale gray pantsuit and matching heels. She'd coiled her icy-blond hair into a bun so tight it looked like a helmet.

As she passed, she grimaced. "Hello, Boo. To what do I owe the pleasure?"

The way she said pleasure made it clear she thought it was anything but.

Before I could answer, a pair of twenty-something men sauntered past us, wetsuits half-unzipped and surfboards at their sides. They gave Cornelia a wide berth and me a lazy nod before disappearing down the sidewalk in a trail of seawater and sand.

I straightened my jacket and stood. "I was hoping we could talk inside."

Cornelia rolled her eyes and started toward the door. "If you're here to complain about the article in today's paper, don't bother. We did the best we could, considering your candidate didn't even bother to show up."

I froze. "He never came by?"

So much for pretending I was on top of things.

Cornelia gave me a sideways glance. "No, and if he won't make the case for why he should be Laguna Bay's mayor, my advisory board can't read his mind." She paused as if considering what she'd just said. Then she shrugged. "Well, most of them can't. But that's not the point. If he doesn't want to act like a motivated candidate, why should we treat him like one?"

I scrambled for something—anything—that might redeem him, but I came up empty. Still, it didn't feel fair.

"You've known Merle forever. There's nothing he could say you don't already know. Maybe he didn't show because he figured you'd already made up your mind."

The words tumbled out, fueled by days of bottled-up frustration.

"Was the fix in from the start?" I snapped. "Wouldn't surprise me. Maybe that's why your own reporter didn't trust this place."

Her keys paused in the lock. "And who exactly are you referring to?"

I leveled my gaze at her. "The dead one."

Her posture stiffened as she pulled the door open. "I don't know what you're talking about, but I suppose you'll enlighten me. That must be why you're here."

She walked in, heels clicking on the floor like exclamation points. "Well, are you coming?"

For all the folklore warning people not to invite vampires into a place, I was beginning to think there should be one about accepting a vampire's invitation as well.

Still, I followed because she was right. That was why I was here.

Cornelia led me straight into her office. As I entered, I had to admit the space was impressive, with big windows and sleek, modern furniture. I declined the offer to sit in either of the clear acrylic chairs positioned in front of her massive white desk, even though my hip was throbbing and my feet weren't faring much better. Standing would make it easier to run if it came to that.

"Suit yourself," she said as she settled into her white leather chair.

A beat later, Zelda appeared in the doorway. "Good morning, Cornelia. I made my famous red velvet cake cookies last night. The ones you love. I figured they would be a nice treat for the staff since it's going to be a long night waiting for election results. Would you like one with your coffee?"

I rubbed my upper lip to hide my smile. A vampire with a soft spot for blood-red cookies? Imagine that.

"Later," Cornelia answered curtly.

Zelda glanced at me, offering nothing, and pulled the door shut.

As it latched, Cornelia dropped the fake smile. "Why are you here, Boo?"

Time to bite the bullet.

"I was thinking about why Fiona didn't keep her notes here," I said. "Why she kept them at home."

Cornelia clasped her hands in front of her, as graceful and threatening as a snake. "She was competitive. I imagine she didn't want any of her colleagues to scoop her story."

"That's what I thought at first too." I took a slow step forward. "Or maybe she didn't trust you. Maybe she thought you were in league with Councilman Dodge, and if he was part of her exposé, maybe she thought you'd kill the story."

Cornelia's back straightened against the tufted white leather. "That's an interesting accusation. Do you have evidence?"

"Not yet," I said.

Her lips twitched, but not in amusement.

I crossed my arms. "Were you hiding something about the Channel Hotel fire? Is that why you killed Fiona? Maybe something that would hurt Councilman Dodge's chances in the election?"

The accusation hit its mark.

"How dare you," she snapped. I half expected her to flash her fangs and lunge at my throat—but she stayed seated, eyes locked on me in a glare that could scorch wallpaper.

"I've protected this community for years. Decades, really. And, yes, I've suppressed stories—but not for myself. For all of us, Boo. Do you have any idea how close we come to being exposed on a fairly regular basis?"

I didn't answer.

She didn't wait.

"Landon Fields? The wolf attacks? The mayor claimed she saw something unnatural—and I buried it. Do you think a human-owned paper would have done that? I don't even like Tom Dodge, but I let him think I support him. It's basic survival."

She leaned forward, eyes blazing. "So, no. I did not kill Fiona, even if she was a constant thorn in my side."

"Then where were you after the town hall?" I demanded.

Her cold eyes fixed me like a bug on a board. "If you must know, I was with the councilman. Tom invited me to dine with him at Amigos Restaurant. He spent the evening pressuring me to announce the *Gazette*'s endorsement of him immediately. For two hours, I had to listen to him drone on about how it was beneath him to be on a ballot with two amateurs. His words, not mine. Apparently, running alongside amateurs was making his investors nervous. I let him believe I was considering it, but that was only to appease him. As I'm sure you saw in today's paper, the *Gazette* endorsed no one."

I should have known that. Maybe if I'd had more than a wink of sleep in the last thirty-six hours, I would have thought to pick up a copy. I wasn't sure what a non-endorsement would mean for Merle's campaign, but I knew what it meant for my suspicions about who killed Fiona.

There was a knock on the door.

Zelda again.

"Councilman Dodge is on the line," she chirped. "He says it's urgent. Shall I put him through?"

Cornelia glanced at me, but I was already inching toward the door.

"You should take it," I said. "We're done here."

Zelda gave me a smug grin as I walked by her.

Outside, I pulled out my phone and called the only place that could confirm Cornelia's story.

"Amigos Restaurant. Alma speaking. How may I help you?"

Alma Gomez's family had been running Amigos Restaurant almost as long as I'd been running the Boo-tique. They were normies, but I'd always considered them friends. Alma also made the best pozole verde I'd ever had. It was making me hungry just thinking about it—probably because I'd skipped breakfast in my morning rush.

"Alma, it's Boo." Once we got the pleasantries out of the way, I asked her my question. "Did Cornelia Sloane and Councilman Dodge have dinner at your place last night?"

"They were here. They ate in our private room. The councilman insisted on it. I tried to tell him that space is only for special events and private parties, but he wouldn't listen. He said they needed privacy."

Why didn't that surprise me?

"What time were they there?" I asked, still clinging to a shred of hope.

"From four to six. Maybe a little later."

That hope fizzled out. I'd already found Fiona by then.

"Are you sure? Could it have been earlier?"

"No. I served them myself. Why?"

"Just curious," I said, my heart sinking. "Thanks, Alma. I'll see you soon."

I ended the call and fought the urge to scream. If Cornelia and Councilman Dodge were both at the restaurant, neither of them could've killed Fiona. I was back at square one—no prime suspects, no answers.

My phone buzzed.

Blocked number.

I hesitated, then picked up.

A muffled voice whispered, "Stop digging, Boo. Or you'll end up like Fiona."

Click.

My hand tightened around the phone until my knuckles ached. I glanced up and down the street—nothing but foggy shop windows, a seagull picking at a discarded fry, and the reminder that Fiona's killer was still out there—and, apparently, watching me.

Chapter 22

Good Intentions

THE KETTLE WHISTLED, SHARP and sudden, and my nerves jumped like they hadn't slept in two days—which, to be fair, wasn't far from the truth.

I yanked the water off the burner and muttered, "Just one peaceful cup of tea. That's all I'm asking. Please."

The sun streamed through the window over the kitchen sink, casting a golden glow on the tile counter and the vase of lavender Delphine had arranged in a mason jar. You'd think, coupled with the soft rustle of leaves outside, might calm me down.

You'd think.

But I was still wound tighter than the spring on our garden gate.

I poured the hot water over the lemon-chamomile tea bag in my favorite mug—the one with the gray tabby cat painted on the side alongside the words "Purr More, Hiss Less." I tried to relax.

Del sat at the table in a loose cotton robe, its green paisley hem pooling at her feet, poking half-heartedly at her bowl of almond-milk yogurt topped with strawberries and granola like she had other things on her mind. "Something's bothering you, Boo. Are you going to tell me what it is, or do I have to guess?"

"You should have stopped me from going to see Cornelia," I grumbled.

Del half choked, half scoffed. "I seem to remember trying to do exactly that. But why? What happened?"

I lifted my cup and blew gently across the surface. "I really thought I was onto something, but I only made things worse."

Del's spoon dangled between her fingers. "That bad?"

"Oh, you know, just your average Tuesday morning—sunshine, songbirds, and me spectacularly offending Laguna Bay's most powerful vampire."

She winced. "Ouch."

I dropped into the chair opposite her and set down the mug, waiting for the tea to steep. "I thought I had her. Marched right into the *Gazette* and accused her of murdering Fiona because she's in league with that twit Tom Dodge."

Del's eyes widened. "You didn't."

"I did. And she has an airtight alibi. She was at Amigos Restaurant."

Del bit her lower lip. "You're sure?"

"I checked with Alma myself. Cornelia was in the restaurant's back room making deals with Dodge at the same time Fiona was meeting her end in the alley. The exact same time, Del."

Her spoon hovered over the yogurt. "So that alibi applies to Councilman Dodge too?"

I dropped my head back and stared at the ceiling. "You bet it does. Two strikes, just like that. Like I said, my whole plan backfired."

A tiny, imperious huff came from the hallway. Then our resident feline sauntered toward the table. Kheppy, apparently refreshed from her nap on my bed, padded in like a queen inspecting her court. She gazed at us with those ancient, amber eyes, stretched luxuriously, and hopped onto the table like she owned the place.

"Hello, Sleepyhead," I said, forcing a smile. "Did we wake you?"

Kheppy sniffed Delphine's yogurt and wrinkled her nose before settling herself in a neat loaf position between us. "You did not wake me, but I heard you say you fired back at the vampire. That is not wise. Her advanced age makes her as immune to flames as she is to sunlight."

I pinched the bridge of my nose and breathed through my frustration. "Backfire means my plan didn't work. I failed."

Kheppy glanced away. "You should have said that."

I swallowed hard. "Noted."

Del, in a gentle voice that usually meant she was about to overstep with good intentions, pushed her bowl aside. "At least now you can stop worrying about it. You've ruled them out. Do you think you should call the detective and tell him what you've discovered?"

I bit back the retort perched on my tongue.

Sure, I could tell the detective. And while I was at it, I could mention the poltergeist haunting my shop—the one who'd tipped me off—and how our little coven of witches had already tried and failed to reason with that cranky spirit. But the moment Detective Ernie Platt started nosing around, who knew how far down that particular rabbit hole he'd dig?

Instead, I smiled and nodded. "You're right, Del. I should do that." But I wouldn't.

Her face softened, clearly pleased, and I hated lying to her, even when it was a white lie.

I didn't mention the call—the one that still echoed in the back of my mind. Del didn't need that weight on her shoulders, not when she was already worrying about the garden and the ghost and my general unraveling. Besides, what would I even say? *Hey, someone with a voice like freezer burn told me to stop snooping, or I'd end up like Fiona.* No thanks. I'd keep that particular nightmare to myself.

I pushed back from the table and gathered my tea, cradling it like it was liquid salvation. "Right now, I need to get some sleep. My hip's aching, my feet feel like I'm walking on spikes, and I can hardly keep my eyes open. I'm going to take this into my room and try to get some rest before Merle's party tonight, which has been moved to his place, by the way."

Del took her bowl to the sink. "Good plan. I think I'll get some work done in the garden before I get ready. The rosemary needs to be trimmed back, and the mint is threatening a takeover."

"Good luck with that," I mumbled as I made my way toward my bedroom.

I grabbed my *Hocus Focus* notebook off the counter as I passed, thinking I'd jot down a few thoughts about Cornelia and Tom's alibis, hoping it might shake loose an idea about what to do next.

The moment I stepped into my room and the cool air hit me—along with the faint scent of rosewater and whatever else was in Del's latest homemade pillow spray—my body voted for sleep instead.

Kheppy slipped in behind me.

I glanced down as she brushed by my ankles. "Are you sure you want to be in here? I might be out for a while. Once I close this door, you'll be stuck."

She leaped onto the bed, circled once, and curled right into the center of the pillows. "I never mind being stuck with you, Boo."

Something inside me cracked a little. The good kind of crack—like a hard shell breaking away.

I set my mug on the nightstand and eased onto the bed beside her, the mattress creaking beneath my tired limbs. I'd been holding myself up with adrenaline and indignation for so long, I'd almost forgotten how it felt to let go.

Kheppy scooted closer, resting her chin on my chest with a deep, contented purr that vibrated right down my bones.

"You're a treasure, you know that?" I murmured, my fingers trailing over the soft fur between her ears.

As I lay there, the tension in my shoulders finally eased. Not because I had answers. I didn't. If anything, I had fewer than ever. But I had this moment. The warmth of my bed, the solid weight of Kheppy against me, the soft whistle of the breeze in the distance, and the rhythmic clink of Del's shears in the garden.

The last few days had been filled with chaos, secrets, and death. But here, now, none of it mattered. I wasn't a sleuth or a campaign manager or even a shopkeeper.

I was just Boo.

For a few sweet, fleeting moments, that was enough.

Chapter 23

Shattered Glass

A BONE-JARRING CRASH SHATTERED the stillness.

I jolted upright in bed, heart hammering, every nerve snapping to attention like someone had dropped me into a fire drill. Kheppy launched off my chest with an indignant yowl and landed on the floor in a blur of gray fur.

"Glass," I said aloud, already scrambling to my feet. "That was glass."

The bedroom was dark except for the silver wash of moonlight streaming through the sheers. My legs protested as I swung them off the mattress, but adrenaline overruled the ache. Operating on autopilot, I grabbed my fuzzy blue robe from the back of the door and threw it on, never mind that I was still in the jeans and T-shirt I'd worn when I'd fallen asleep. I bolted for the kitchen, bare feet slapping against the linoleum floor.

Delphine was already standing near the refrigerator, both hands covering her mouth. The pale yellow walls looked ghostly in the silver light mixed with the porch glow. At her feet, a glittering sprawl of smashed glass caught the light like a constellation of tiny stars.

In the middle of the mess sat a rock the size of a fist. A note was rubber-banded around it.

I stopped just shy of the scattered shards, the cool breeze wafting in brisk against my skin. "Are you okay?"

Del nodded mutely, eyes locked on the floor. "I was rinsing lettuce. It nearly hit me."

I slipped on my Birkenstocks, which I'd left near the door, and crossed to her slowly. "Did you read the note?"

She shook her head. "I didn't want to touch it. It might be evidence."

Of course she was thinking like a crime show detective. I crouched, avoiding the shards, and pulled the note free.

A threat, scribbled in thick black marker, stared back at me: *Stop badgering Cornelia—or else!*

There was a smear at the bottom—deep red, slightly smudged.

I blanched. "Is that blood?"

I dropped the note like it burned.

Kheppy crept in behind me and sniffed. "Not blood," she announced. "Chocolate."

Del and I looked at each other, then back at Kheppy.

I lifted the note again—more carefully this time—and smelled it. Kheppy was right. I caught a distinctly sweet scent of chocolate—red-velvet chocolate, it would seem—along with a heady dose of déjà vu.

The intruder at Fiona's place—the one I'd knocked over while escaping—had smelled the same.

My skin prickled with goosebumps. "I smelled this at Fiona's place."

Del frowned. "Are you sure?"

"Positive." I looked past her, out the broken window. The garden beyond was bathed in moonlight, all silvery outlines and shadowy silhouettes. "Whoever threw that rock did it from out there. Did you hear a car?"

"No. I was here at the sink, washing the romaine," she said. "I'd just opened the refrigerator when it happened. Nearly scared me out of my mind."

That explained why a head of lettuce was sitting under the table.

I moved to the screen door and gazed out. It was too dark to see anything clearly. "Stay here," I said, pushing my way onto the porch.

"Boo, wait!" Del's voice was charged with alarm. "Don't go out there!"

Kheppy slid by me and jumped onto the porch railing. "Where are you going?"

"I'll be fine," I muttered, evading her question. "Protect Del." Then I set off to confirm what I suspected.

The breeze smelled of damp soil and roses, and the cicadas had gone eerily silent. My Birkenstocks scraped lightly against the flagstone path. Beyond the garden beds and trellises, I saw movement—a dark figure slipping through the yard, trying to blend into the shadows.

"Hey!" I shouted. "Stop! I'm making a citizen's arrest!"

As soon as the words left my mouth, I mentally smacked myself. I didn't know anything about citizen's arrests. Did they even exist outside of the movies? I made a mental note to add it to the list of questions to answer later.

My threat didn't stop the dark figure creeping along the edge of our property. Instead, it sent the person running for the hill behind the garden fence.

I took off in pursuit, legs screaming in protest. Birkenstocks weren't built for speed, and after fifty yards of awkward clomping over uneven ground, I was gasping and wheezing like a poor excuse for a tea kettle.

I bent over, hands on my knees, and tried to catch my breath.

Then something shot past me.

Fast. Silent. And far larger than the occasional bunny rabbits and squirrels we often saw in the neighborhood.

Fear flooded through me. Was it a wolf? A werewolf? We'd reached an understanding with the Landon pack, or so I'd thought.

I jerked my head up. No, it wasn't something canine. It was a massive tiger with silver-gray fur that bounded across the lawn with impossible grace.

"Kheppy," I breathed.

She didn't look back. Just lunged at the running figure, who shrieked and stumbled before crashing to the ground in a tangle of limbs and cries. Kheppy pinned her prey easily, her enormous paws pressing into the figure's shoulders.

By the time I hobbled up, chest heaving and pulse thudding in my ears, I could see the familiar culprit staring into Kheppy's eyes.

Kheppy leaned down, her tawny gaze narrowing. "Look at me," she intoned, her voice deep and threaded with ancient power.

The woman on the ground went still. Eyes wide. Face slack.

I tried to catch my breath as I stepped closer, heart slamming in my chest.

The culprit, dressed in black leggings and a matching hoodie, with a curly lock of hair peeking out from beneath the hood, was unmistakable.

Zelda Harcourt.

Still shaking with adrenaline, I planted my hands on my hips and leaned over, searching Zelda's dazed stare for any hint of recognition. What was going through her mind? Did she even understand what had happened to her? I didn't know, but I knew this: I was finally going to get some answers.

Chapter 24
Paws-itive Reinforcement

KHEPPY'S MASSIVE PAW WAS planted squarely on Zelda Harcourt's chest, pinning her to the dusty canyon hillside like a striped, muscle-bound paperweight. Zelda's eyes were open but unfocused, blinking slow and dreamy—like someone caught between waking and sleep. Her black hoodie had slipped back, revealing sweat-slicked hair plastered in damp strands across her forehead.

The only sound was the rhythmic rasp of crickets and the whistle of the wind through the surrounding chaparral. Twilight had come and gone, and now the world was bathed in that deep indigo hue that made everything feel both magical and just a little frightening.

"You made that look way too easy," I said to Kheppy, still bent over with my hands on my knees, trying to catch my breath.

My now tiger-sized friend didn't so much as glance my way, but her tail twitched with unmistakable pride. "I've been practicing. At night. While you slept."

I straightened. "Wait—that's why you've been sneaking out?"

Another flick of the tail. "The backyard has excellent shadows at night and fewer interruptions."

I chuckled softly and shook my head. "I should probably be mad at you for not telling me what you were doing, but honestly, I'm kind of impressed."

She glanced back over her shoulder, eyes gleaming. "As you should be."

I took another deep breath, straightened, and looked down at Zelda. "Is she okay?"

"She is not hurt," Kheppy replied. "I have calmed her mind."

I squinted. "You mean you hypnotized her?"

Kheppy's broad shoulders rolled in a slow-motion shrug. "Yes. I suppose that is what I have done."

Now that I'd caught my breath, I tried to figure out what to do next. "How long will it last?"

"I do not know." Her ears flicked. "I do not always know what will happen when I shift—or when I use my gifts. I require more practice."

That surprised me. I'd always thought of Kheppy as having all the answers, the all-knowing ancient cat who could quote the Egyptian Book of the Dead and tick off historical facts like she was the Encyclopedia Britannica. But hearing her admit she was still figuring out this recently discovered skill? That was new.

"Good to know," I murmured. "I guess we're all winging it tonight."

I crouched beside Zelda and stared into her glazed-over eyes. "Let's see if I can get her to talk." Up close, a cloying sweetness curled into my nose—chocolate, not blood. The same scent that stained the note and clung to the intruder at Fiona's place. I cleared my throat. "Zelda, why are you here?"

Zelda blinked once. She seemed to focus on me. "Boo? Is that you?"

"Yes," I said, keeping my voice calm even as my patience frayed. I had a dozen questions but started with the most important. "Why did you break into Fiona's place? Why were you there?"

Her eyelids fluttered. Her tone distant but steady. "Those files," she murmured. "I needed them—had to be sure Fiona didn't have anything that could embarrass Cornelia."

My stomach tightened. "Embarrass her how?"

"I protect her," she whispered, her voice still lost in trance.

A chill slipped down my spine at the devotion in her voice. I glanced at Kheppy, who was watching silently, tail flicking. "Zelda," I pressed, "did you kill Fiona?"

"No," she said simply.

Well, that was a relief. Or it would have been, if she hadn't followed it up with:

"I would have, though."

I froze. "What? Why?"

Her expression remained distant, almost blissful. "Fiona was a problem for Cornelia," she murmured, her voice soft and detached. "If I could take away the problem, maybe Cornelia would make me."

I leaned back, heart thudding. "Make you what?"

Zelda's lips curled into something that might have passed for a smile but gave me the creeps. "Make me like her."

She emphasized her, which sent a shiver down my spine. I hoped she didn't mean what I thought she meant. "Why? What do you think she is?"

That creepy, vacant smile widened. "A vampire." She breathed the word reverently. "She's the most powerful vampire in the world."

I snorted. "I wouldn't go that far," I muttered, casting a glance at Kheppy. "Someone has been watching too many *Twilight* movies."

But then Zelda gave this look—one of those far-off, euphoric expressions that usually came after too many glasses of chardonnay. "I want to be a vampire. More than anything."

"Well, isn't that peachy?" I mumbled, scrubbing a hand over my face. "What is it with normies and vampires?"

Her words stuck in my head, refusing to settle. If Zelda knew what Cornelia was, what else did she know? Did she know about the rest of us? Delphine, me, and the other garden witches? Merle and Rupert? The whole supernatural enchilada?

I opened my mouth to ask, but a rustling on the path behind us made me twist around. My whole body tensed until I spotted the silhouette of someone stumbling forward, panting and muttering under her breath.

Del.

She stomped out of the darkness like a grumpy wood nymph in orthopedic shoes, one hand clutching her phone and the other waving off a low-hanging branch. Her gray braids had picked up bits of dried weeds. Her sweater looked like she'd wrestled a scarecrow.

"I swear to everything green and growing," she wheezed, "this path gets steeper every day. Boo, your phone wouldn't stop ringing, so I answered it. You need to take it."

I glared at her. "I'm a little busy at the moment."

Between gasps, she said, "I know, but take it. Trust me."

Apparently no wasn't an option. "Who is it?"

"Merle," she said. Then, into the receiver: "Here she is." She passed the phone to me with a look that said she was holding me personally responsible for making her hike up the hill like a billy goat.

I grimaced as I took the phone. "I'm kind of in the middle of something. Can I call you—"

"Boo," Merle said. Serious. Flat. No trace of his usual playful drawl. "This is important."

My sass deflated like a failed soufflé. "Okay. What happened?"

"Rupert's been talking to Fiona."

My stomach did a weird little flip. "Of course he has," I murmured. "And?"

"We're at the Channel Hotel site," he said. "You need to get over here."

I opened my mouth to refuse—a reflex, really—but something in his tone stopped me. Whatever it was, it was big.

"Give me a few minutes," I said. "I have to sort out some things first."

"Just hurry."

Click.

I turned back to Del, who was leaning over Kheppy's enormous striped shoulder. "Is that Zelda Harcourt?"

"Yeah," I said and filled her in on what she'd missed, including Zelda's ridiculous Twilight fantasy. "Will you help me get her back to our place? The last thing we need is her running to an emergency room and claiming she was attacked by a tiger. That's not the kind of news story we need."

Del arched an eyebrow. "But she was attacked by a tiger."

"Not attacked. Just stopped," I said. "Big difference."

"I suppose so," Del said, trying to reach her back to brush away the twigs that were clinging there. "Can you help me get these off? I think they have thorns."

I turned her around and picked off the dried bits of vegetation clinging where she couldn't reach. When I was done, I turned back to find a gray fluff ball curled on Zelda's chest, her tail tucked around her body, fast asleep.

I stared. "Guess that was it for tiger mode."

Del shot me a sideways glance. "She was a tiger, right? Tell me that wasn't just low blood sugar messing with my head."

"Oh, she was a tiger," I reassured her.

"Talk about *paws-itive* reinforcement," Del said and giggled at her joke.

"Very funny," I said. "She was gentle with Zelda, but she could have done some major damage if she'd wanted to."

Del muttered something under her breath about needing more chamomile tea—a lot more. Honestly, I didn't blame her. But I wasn't sure there was enough tea on the planet to settle either of us tonight. And deep down, I had a sinking feeling that I hadn't seen the worst of it yet.

Chapter 25

Hole Affair

By the time I rolled up to the charred ruins of the Channel Hotel, the sky had turned a dark, inky blue. Kheppy sat primly in the passenger seat, nose pressed to the window to watch the passing landscape. Every once in a while, her whiskers twitched with interest.

"Why on earth did Merle want to meet out here?" I muttered mostly to myself. The abandoned lot was cordoned off by a chain-link fence and crammed with weeds, shadows, and a hefty supply of foreboding. "And where is he?"

Kheppy didn't respond, just stared out the window like she was waiting for something.

"Do you see his truck?" I asked.

Then I noticed it, around the back and partially hidden by a leaning eucalyptus tree and a battered old trash bin. I pulled up alongside it and parked.

After I killed the engine, I scooped up Kheppy. She offered no resistance and curled against me like a warm loaf of purring bread, soft and humming against my chest. Her breath stirred the hair by my collar as I carefully navigated the loose gravel toward the fence.

A gap caught my eye. A section of the chain-link had been clipped and peeled back like a tin can's lid, creating an opening wide enough for a person to slip through. I crouched and waddled through, shoes crunching on dead grass.

Voices rose above the distant traffic and singing crickets. Or rather, one voice—Merle's.

"You could ask her to be a little more specific," he was saying, his tone a blend of frustration and fatigue.

I couldn't see Rupert, of course—usually nobody could, except Merle—but I could tell by the way he paused that he wasn't just thinking out loud. Ghost conversations had a rhythm to them. And I recognized this one.

"Once, sure," he continued. "Twice, fine. But this is our third hole."

I moved closer and cleared my throat. "I'm here. What's so important that you couldn't tell me over the phone, and why do you look like you've been crawling through a trench when you should be hosting an election party?"

Merle's hands—and the sleeves of his flannel shirt—were so caked with dirt, he looked like he'd been in a mud-wrestling match, not preparing to win the city's top office.

He wiped the sweat and grime from his forehead with the back of his hand. "Sissy's at my place. She swung by earlier to help with the party preparations, and we've still got time. The polls don't close for another hour, and counting the ballots will take even longer."

It was great that Sissy was holding down the fort, but nobody was going to Merle's election night party to see her. I shifted Kheppy to the other arm. "I don't know much about campaign strategy, but I'm pretty sure this isn't the best use of your time."

He offered a crooked smile, then glanced at Kheppy. "You brought backup."

"Uncertain times," I said with a shrug. "Actually, it was Del's idea. She made the excellent point that you were asking me to meet you in an abandoned lot with a killer on the loose. I figured I should at least bring some protection."

Merle chuckled. "So, you brought a cat?"

I stared down at the gray fluff ball. "You'd be surprised how fierce she can be. Not at the moment, of course, but trust me. Nobody is going to mess with her or me." Merle didn't know about Kheppy's tiger-sized alter ego. I probably should have told him, but something was telling me to keep it quiet for now.

"Fair point." He tried to brush away the dirt clinging to his sleeves, but it only made it worse.

"So," I prompted, shifting Kheppy slightly so her claws didn't snag my sweater, "what are you doing out here when you should be working on your acceptance speech or something?"

His smile faded. "Let's not get ahead of ourselves. You don't know if I'm going to win this thing."

"You're right. I don't. I just can't imagine who would think Tom Dodge would ever put Laguna Bay's concerns over his own."

"You don't know that, Boo," he said. There was a gentle rebuke in his tone, but I wasn't sorry. If Merle didn't see it, it was because he was so kindhearted, he could only see the best in people. "But can we put the election aside for a minute?"

"Fine," I groused.

"Rupert and I came out here because he's been trying to figure out why Fiona hasn't moved on. The thing is, she doesn't seem to remember. Rupert thought being here might jog her memory. It took some coaxing, but he finally got her to leave the shop and make it out this way."

I hated giving Rupert credit for a good idea, but this one actually made sense. "Has she remembered anything?"

"I think so." Merle motioned for me to follow him toward a patch of ground nearby. "She keeps circling this spot," he said, gesturing to the open space behind what used to be the Channel Hotel. "Rupert says she keeps repeating, 'Here, here, it's here.' Over and over. But that's all we've gotten from her."

"So you started digging?" I asked.

He shrugged. "Rupert and I both kind of felt something," he said. "Something is buried here. And I don't mean old pipes or scrap metal. It's something... significant."

He led me to a fresh hole in the earth. About three feet deep and five feet long, with a shovel stood upright in one corner. He grabbed a flashlight from his back pocket and switched it on. "There might be something here because Fiona started going wild when I started digging here. I'd just hit something when you pulled up and was about to take a look."

I leaned in.

The beam of light cut through the darkness. It snagged on something in the soil.

I jumped into the pit for a closer look.

In an instant, Merle was beside me.

"Is that..." I didn't finish the question because he was right. This wasn't old pipes or scrap metal. This was bone. A skull, if I wasn't mistaken.

He kneeled, one hand steadying the flashlight for a better view, while the other brushed away the dirt.

I set Kheppy gently on the ground and crouched beside him, helping to clear the soil from around the figure. The hair was long gone. The skin, too. Only bones remained, and the remnants of bright turquoise fabric. The synthetic fibers had melted at the edges and burned black. As we uncovered more of it, it became clear the fabric was part of a silky blazer. As I brushed the dirt away from the skeleton's shoulders, I felt foam beneath the fabric. Shoulder pads, and they were big enough to make a linebacker blush. Something deep in my gut twisted.

Could this be...?

No. I kept digging, trying to unearth a different answer.

Merle must've felt the familiarity too. He rocked back on his heels and let out a heavy sigh. "I recognize this jacket. I'll bet you do too."

"No, Merle. Don't say it." I shook my head, the words barely a whisper. "It can't be her."

But denial never stopped the truth.

"This is Maureen," he whispered.

And the sorrow in his voice broke what little hope I had left.

"But how?" I wailed. "How could she have been here all this time?"

For thirty years, we'd all believed she'd run away, and she'd never gone anywhere.

She'd been here all along.

"I think someone killed her," Merle said, crouching beside the skull and angling his flashlight toward the back of the head. I leaned in for a better view, and my stomach flipped—the crack was unmistakable.

Kheppy jumped down and padded closer, her gaze fixed on the broken skull. She stood still for a long beat, then turned to me.

"I will allow it," she said softly, her voice calm but solemn. "I submit freely."

Before I could ask what she meant or who she was talking to, her body went stiff. Her tawny eyes flared bright green, glowing unnaturally in the shadows—and then they weren't her eyes anymore.

Fiona's voice came out of Kheppy's mouth—unnatural, distorted, and echoing with something not entirely of this world. "It's here," she said. "The ring. The fox. It is here."

Merle and I both stumbled back, startled. My heart hammered in my chest.

Then something caught my eye—a glint of something almost covered by the dirty turquoise lapel.

"What's that?" I asked, pointing.

Merle swept his flashlight over the grave again. The beam skimmed something metallic. I bent down, careful not to disturb the fragile remains, and gently nudged aside a few curled finger bones.

It was a large ring—looped through a tarnished chain as though it had been worn as a pendant. I lifted it gently and rubbed the surface with my thumb.

Beneath the grime, an engraving emerged: an animal standing on its hind legs, a bushy tail arched behind it.

"You probably shouldn't touch that," Merle said. "It's evidence."

"I know," I murmured. "But look at this." I held it under his flashlight beam, tilting it so the image caught the light.

The Voss family crest.

Merle exhaled slowly. "That belonged to Charles Voss."

"Then why was it around Maureen's neck?"

He shook his head. "It looks valuable. Maybe she stole it. Or maybe he gave it to her."

"Why would he do that?"

He rubbed his chin, leaving a long, dirty streak on his face. "Beats me. Maybe he was trying to buy her place. He went on a buying spree about that time, and this property adjoins his."

"Is that why she wanted you to appraise the place? So she could set a sales price?"

He grimaced. "She never mentioned wanting to sell, but I suppose he might have made her an offer. Anything's possible."

I stared at the ring, letting the possibilities churn. "The ring wouldn't be enough to buy the place. This was something else. When a man gives a woman a ring, it usually means something."

"You mean something more than a real estate transaction?"

"Yeah. Do you think they were involved?"

Merle scoffed. "That doesn't sound like Charles Voss. He only ever loved one thing—money."

I didn't know the man well before he died, which was a few years after the fire, but I remembered his reputation. He'd turned his back on the supernatural community to carve a place for himself among the local rich and powerful set. Still, one thing didn't necessarily negate the other.

I glanced at Merle. "Was he the kind of guy who might have faked romantic interest if it might get him a better price?"

Merle didn't answer right away. When he did, his voice was tight. "It wouldn't surprise me. There wasn't much that man wouldn't do to get what he wanted."

I stared at Maureen's remains and that ring. "It meant something to her. She wore it. Protected it. Why?"

Merle's voice dropped. "Rupert doesn't know. And Maureen's spirit is gone. She passed on."

"I suppose that's a blessing," I whispered. "But all this has to have something to do with Fiona's murder. It has to."

I checked my watch. "The polling places are about to close. We need to get you back to the party."

He appeared torn. "We can't leave her like this."

He was right. "Can Rupert watch over her until the police arrive? They're about to receive an interesting anonymous call."

For a moment, I thought he might refuse. But then he turned to the space beside him and had a whispered conversation. When he turned back to me, he said, "Rupert will stay. He's trying to explain it to Fiona, but he thinks it will take some time."

"She's still here?" I asked.

He nodded.

I picked up Kheppy, who had fallen fast asleep after Fiona had spoken through her. I cuddled her close as Merle and I walked back to the opening in the fence.

Neither of us spoke as we climbed into our vehicles. I waited for Merle to leave first, then followed him down the narrow access road.

As I drove, something tugged at me. A feeling.

Not a vision. Not a voice. Just... a sense. If anyone knew why Maureen was clutching that ring, I had a pretty good idea who that person was.

I flicked on my blinker and turned down a different street.

Just one quick stop, I told myself.

Chapter 26

Underdressed

My Karmann Ghia's headlights sliced through the fog as I curved up the narrow road that snaked behind the Channel Hotel ruins. Kheppy sat in the passenger seat, her tail tucked around her paws. Neither of us spoke. We didn't have to. The image of Maureen Calvert's skeletal hand still burned into my brain—the way it clutched that silver ring with the fox crest, as if it held the truth of what had happened that night.

Perhaps it did.

When I made the sudden turn onto the small lane, I didn't know exactly what I intended to do, but my gut told me I had to do something.

As the wildland gave way to a lush, manicured landscape, I knew I was in the right place. The Voss estate held answers, I was sure of it.

Nestled in the foothills behind the Channel Hotel property, the mansion peeked out between thick rows of magnolia trees and towering eucalyptus. The lavish Italianate home had archways, a rotunda, and nearly as much marble as the Parthenon, and right now it was lit up like a carnival at night.

The election party Eleanor was throwing for Tom Dodge was apparently in full swing.

The estate's wrought-iron gates were opened wide, with a valet kiosk set up nearby. A line of expensive cars idled along the cobblestone driveway, like shiny beetles headed for the hive. I pulled up behind a silver coupe and smiled over my stuck window as a kid in a red blazer approached. He looked about sixteen, with a wispy mustache that fooled no one.

"Good evening," he said with a grin. "Here for the victory party?"

Of course Eleanor wouldn't wait for the official results before crowning her candidate the winner. I bit back a sigh and glanced down at my dirt-smudged jeans and the purple *What's Up Witches* tee—perfectly acceptable for ghost hunting at the Channel Hotel, less so for crashing a high-society soirée. Would Eleanor mind me tracking mud into her palace with my Birkenstocks? Almost certainly. Did I care? Not even a little.

I smiled sweetly. "That's right. The victory party."

He nodded and gestured toward the lane. "Pull up behind the Bentley, ma'am. An attendant will be right with you."

"Thanks," I said and inched forward in line.

Kheppy turned her fiery eyes on me as I pulled out my phone and typed a text message to Merle: *Making a quick stop. Be there soon. Make sure you have plenty of chips and dip for the party.*

Kheppy was still glaring when I hit *Send*.

"Don't judge me," I muttered. "I'm figuring it out as I go."

"You could figure it out in the morning," she said, her voice low and dripping with disapproval. "After you've showered, and slept, and maybe come to your senses."

"This won't take long."

She rolled her feline shoulders. "Great last words."

"I think you mean famous last words," I corrected. "And you may be right, but it's too late to turn back now."

I caught my reflection in the rearview mirror and tried to tame the blue frizz haloing my head. One particularly stubborn curl sprang defiantly upward. I pressed it flat. Good enough.

As we neared the front of the line, Kheppy sprang into the back and disappeared beneath the passenger seat.

"You're not coming in with me?" I asked.

"That is correct," came her reply from the shadows.

"Fine. I can handle this on my own."

I hadn't expected her to join me, but now that I was seconds from stepping inside alone, the weight of it was settling in.

The valet opened my door and did his best to hide a wince at my appearance. I handed him the key with a cheerful smile. "Don't worry about the open window. It's broken."

"Yes, ma'am," he said and handed me the yellow claim slip.

"Don't take it far," I said. "I'll only be a few minutes."

"No problem. Enjoy your evening," he said with a customer-service smile.

As I stepped away and watched him climb in, I bit back the urge to warn him about the cat under the seat. Kheppy knew how to behave around normies, though. It was probably best to leave it alone. That's what I told myself as I headed toward the mansion.

Besides, I had enough to worry about. The prospect of what I was about to do hit me like a tidal wave—the bright lights, elegant laughter, and the nauseating smell of money and influence. Part of me wanted to turn back and hightail it out of there. The other clung as tightly to the memory of Maureen Calvert in that pitiful grave as she had to that silver ring.

And there was Fiona to consider.

"That girl was a pain in the backside," I mumbled to myself. "But she deserves this. They both do."

I straightened, smoothed the front of my shirt, and pointed my muddy Birkenstocks toward the door.

Inside, the foyer looked like something out of a magazine. Marble floors, carved moldings, and a curved staircase. To mark the occasion, red, white, and blue bunting adorned the banister, and a massive banner featuring Tom Dodge's grinning face stared at me from a corner.

A woman in a caterer's uniform offered me a glass of champagne. I waved it off. Boo plus alcohol plus a snooty party equaled trouble.

It was already a heady crowd. I spotted familiar faces from local gallery openings, charity galas, and that local merchants meeting I swore I'd never attend again. They were all clustered in little social hives, swapping compliments and gossip.

As I wandered deeper into the house, I caught sight of Cornelia Sloane locked in conversation with a councilwoman. Cornelia had said she wasn't in league with Tom Dodge, but why else would she be here? Despite occasional nods as the woman in front of her spoke, Cornelia's vampire gaze tracked everything around her. I had to wonder if she knew what her assistant Zelda had been up to. I wasn't going to be the one to tell her. At least not tonight.

Tonight was about Eleanor Voss, and there she was.

In fact, it was impossible to miss her in that flashy silver evening gown as she stood at the center of a cozy circle with Tom at her side. "Someone with vision," she was saying to the others as she placed a palm on his shoulder, "who understands the value of this town. With Tom, we will have a leader who thinks big and sees big things in Laguna Bay's future. We will finally have someone who treats this town like the coastal gem it really is. It's truly an overlooked treasure."

As the sycophants applauded her clearly rehearsed pep talk, my blood pressure spiked. My feet moved before I fully registered what I was doing. A slow simmering rage carried me forward, pushing me through the crowd until I stood directly in front of her.

"Eleanor," I said loudly enough to silence the nearby chatter. "Since you're talking about treasures, I thought you might be interested in one I've just discovered."

She frowned at me, confused, then annoyed. "Boo. I wasn't expecting you."

I bet.

Without missing a beat, I reached into my pocket and pulled out the silver ring, carefully wrapped in a wad of tissues. I held it out to her, the fox crest gleaming under the chandelier's light. "Does this look familiar?" I held it up for her to see. "If I had to guess, I'd say it belonged to your father. What do you think?"

"How should I know?" she snapped.

I found her irritation deeply satisfying. "Do you know where it was? Clutched in the hand of a dead woman, and not just any woman, either. I'm sure you remember Maureen Calvert."

The round of hushed gasps in the room told me at least some of those present recalled the name.

"She used to own the Channel Hotel. People thought she burned it down to collect the insurance money and fled when people died inside. Only it turns out, she didn't flee at all. She was murdered and buried right there on the property, probably that same night."

The crowd fell silent. Eleanor's smile twitched, but she didn't falter. Instead, something dark and dangerous flashed in her eyes.

"My father had nothing to do with that fire or that woman," she said. "I think you should leave." She turned to the back of the room and snapped her fingers.

A mountain of a man stepped away from the wall and walked toward us. He was broad and bald and had a dead-eyed look that made me wonder if anyone was home.

"This woman shouldn't be here," Eleanor said coolly as he approached. "Would you escort her out?"

"Of course, Ms. Voss," he replied.

Before I could protest, his hand was on my arm—gentle but firm.

"Wait a minute." I had more to say, but he was already steering me away.

As he pushed me toward the towering front doors, something caught my eye—a bronze crest mounted above the archway.

The fox.

Upright, tail curled high.

Just like the one on the ring.

My suspicions flared—sharp, undeniable—and gave me just enough fire to wrench my arm free from Eleanor's bodyguard. She could play dumb about the ring, pretend her father had nothing to do with the Channel Hotel or its owner, but I wasn't buying a word of it. If her first instinct was to shut me up, it wasn't because I'd said too much. It was because I'd said exactly what she already knew. The only question left was—had she killed to keep it buried?

My giant escort pushed me past the towering doors and into the cold night air, tinged with sea salt and secrets.

And just like that, I was back outside. Shaken, but not done. Not by a long shot.

Chapter 27

Crash and Clatter

"I CAN SEE MYSELF out, thank you," I snapped, twisting away from the bodyguard's meaty grip.

He muttered something about "annoying party crash-ers," but I didn't catch the rest because I was already storming off, my Birkenstocks smacking against the flag-stones with every righteous step.

"Buddy, you have no idea who you're working for." I scowled at him over my shoulder for good measure.

The air outside Eleanor Voss's mansion was thick with the scent of roast beef and garlicky potatoes from the buffet line the caterers had set up on the patio. I inhaled deeply, trying to push away the sting of embarrassment.

It didn't work. Not only had I been unceremoniously and publicly thrown out in front of Laguna Bay's rich and powerful, I also had to accept the fact that it had gotten me nowhere.

Eleanor's expression revealed nothing when I showed her the silver ring Maureen Calvert had been clutching. A ring that should've made Eleanor lose at least one shade of that perfectly powdered complexion.

But no. She'd sighed, sipped her champagne, and lied through her unnaturally white teeth.

And there was nothing I could do about it.

"I don't have to be a mind reader to know that woman was lying," I mumbled to myself.

The shame prickled worse than a sunburn. I should have pressed harder. I should have asked why Maureen—an assumed arsonist and fugitive—had been buried on her own property without anyone's knowledge, all while clutching a Voss family heirloom. But I'd backed off when that bulldog in a designer dress told me to scram.

I trudged toward the line of cars parked along the cobblestone lane beside the estate. Somewhere among the sports cars and limousines was my Karmann Ghia, hopefully with a cat still inside.

My phone buzzed, and I dug it out of my pocket, thumb already swiping the text message notification before I'd even registered that the sender was Merle.

Where are you? Your sister is here. I told her you were right behind me. She's getting worried. Me, too.

Then, another message from him popped onto the screen:

I hope that's okay.

Those four little words stretched a smile across my face, despite everything.

It surprised me. I didn't like people fussing over me. Never had. I was the one who fixed things, handled things, picked up pieces when others dropped them. That's what being strong and independent meant, right? But knowing that Merle was worried about me felt kind of nice.

And more than that, I was glad he seemed to be as unsure about things as I was. The hesitation in his message made me feel like the awkward, slow-motion spark between us wasn't just a nostalgic whim. Maybe it was something real.

I typed back:

It's more than okay. I'm sorry, but I'm going to be late to the party. Will explain later.

Send.

As soon as the message disappeared into the digital ether, reality snapped back into focus.

My work here wasn't done. Maureen Calvert's body had been hidden for decades, along with an undeniable truth clutched between her fingers. I would bet my last pumpkin spice cupcake that Eleanor, with her steely poise and cold ambition, knew more about that ring and Maureen's attachment to it than she cared to admit.

I glanced up at the glowing mansion on the hillside in front of me. From this angle, it looked like a wedding cake—three tiers of white columns and walls draped in lush ivy. Through the windows, I could make out silhouettes of the party guests—laughing, drinking, and celebrating as if everything were fine.

But the party wouldn't last all night. The guests would leave eventually, and Eleanor would be alone. Then maybe—just maybe—I could pry the truth out of her.

Something told me it had to be now or never.

If I waited, there was no telling what evidence she could make disappear. It would certainly give her time to consult her army of lawyers, who would almost certainly advise her to stay quiet.

I had to do this now, before she could build a defense. Tonight, I might still learn the truth.

I glanced around for any sign of that bald bouncer. None. Good.

As I ducked through a narrow break in the hedge, my jeans caught on a thorny branch. I muttered something foul under my breath, brushed off the snag, and pressed deeper into the underbrush.

The faint crunch of dried leaves gave way to soft dirt as I crept toward the back of the house. I found a small boulder tucked beneath a gnarled tree and brushed it off with the sleeve of my denim jacket before plopping down. A few stray pine needles poked me in the rear, but I didn't move.

I settled in to wait.

And wait.

And...

I must've dozed off. Because the revving of a nearby engine jolted me awake.

I sat upright. My neck cracked, and a cramp pinched my side, but I was instantly alert.

A red Ferrari peeled away from its lone spot along what had been a long row of vehicles. The last guest, apparently. The once-illuminated windows were dark now, save for a few in the back and the porch lanterns glowing like fireflies in shadows.

I checked my phone. Just past midnight.

My window was closing.

I crept along the patio's edge, careful not to knock over any abandoned folding tables or stub my toes on the chairs. The buffet tables were stripped bare.

Then I saw Eleanor.

Her back faced me, one hand cradling a champagne flute, the other draped over the railing. Her chestnut hair, once sculpted into a fashionable French roll, now fell in soft waves over her shoulders. She appeared tired. Exhausted, really.

I waited, listening for any sounds of nearby staff or lingering guests. Nothing but crickets in the distance.

When I was sure it was just the two of us, I stepped out of the shadows and cleared my throat.

She turned slowly, her mouth curled in a tight, sinister smile.

"I distinctly remember telling you to leave, Boo Boudreaux."

"We have unfinished business," I said.

She raised her glass, as if toasting me. "No, dear. I don't think so."

That tone. That annoying, dismissive tone.

It lit something inside me.

I marched toward her. No more games. "Do you know what really happened the night of the fire? Maureen Calvert didn't run off. She was buried in her own backyard. How in the world could the emergency responders miss that?"

Eleanor didn't flinch. Just tilted her head. "You are persistent. I'll give you that."

"Persistent?" I repeated, my voice rising. "Maureen died clutching your father's ring. Doesn't that seem strange? Doesn't it raise questions for you? Or do you already know the answers?"

She let out a small, derisive laugh. "Why don't you mind your own business, Boo? If you know what's good for you, you'll stick to your weird little Halloween shop and leave the rest of us alone."

I scoffed. "You've known me long enough to know I don't appreciate threats." I pulled my phone from my pocket. "Maybe it would be better if we called the police and let them sort it out."

I didn't want to call the police. I just wanted to scare her. The fire behind her eyes told me I'd done a lot more than that.

"Do you think the police—or anyone—will believe the word of a senile old woman over the heir to the Voss family fortune?" She sneered the hurtful words.

Senile? Old? I told myself she was just trying to get under my skin and did my best to rise above the insults. "I do, actually," I said, steeling myself against her insults. "Shall we test the theory?"

That's when it happened.

Her hand snapped up—*bam!*—a white-blue lightning bolt shot from her fingertips and knocked the phone out of my hand. As it flew across the patio, a second streak hit my shoulder. The pain landed a second later.

My knees buckled. My vision went starburst-white, and my arms flailed as I fell backward, crashing against a tray table, sending an abandoned champagne flute clattering beside me, shattering into a spray of glass.

The scent of ozone singed my nose, and every nerve in my body buzzed. I stared up at her from the ground, stunned.

Eleanor stepped forward, her heels clicking against the stones, her silver gown rippling like liquid mercury.

"Let me be perfectly clear," she said, her voice colder than the magic she'd just thrown at me. "You don't want to know what I'm capable of, and you certainly don't want to test me again."

She turned her back on me like I wasn't even worth another look.

But as I struggled to sit upright, gripping the edge of a chair for support, one thing was certain.

The rumors about the Voss family abandoning their magic?

Greatly exaggerated.

As the wind whispered through the trees and the burn of Eleanor's magic still pulsed under my skin like an old bruise, another thought hit me hard:

She was scared—because if I were just some harmless shopkeeper, she wouldn't have zapped me like a bug.

I pushed myself to my feet, shaky but standing, fueled by nothing more than grit and the sheer refusal to let that witch have the last word.

Then—*snap*.

A rustle behind me.

I froze. My breath caught in my throat.

Another step. The soft snap of twigs and dead leaves underfoot.

Not my imagination. Someone—or *something*—was creeping closer.

A fresh wave of fear surged through me—hot, prickly, and electric—until I caught a glimpse of Eleanor's face.

She'd looked so arrogant before. But now?

That look on her face was sheer terror.

Whatever was behind me wasn't part of her plan.

I clenched my fists, bracing myself, and turned to face whatever had her so rattled.

Chapter 28

The Patio

"WELL, AREN'T YOU A sight for sore eyes," I said, more relieved than I cared to admit.

Kheppy, in all her majestic tiger glory, stood behind me like an ancient guardian, muscles taut beneath silver and black stripes, amber eyes gleaming with purpose. Her ears twitched at my voice. A big, knowing grin curled across her whiskered face before she turned to Eleanor Voss.

Eleanor, on the other hand, was unraveling faster than a cheap sweater in a hot dryer.

"Do you see that? Tell me you see that!" she screeched, staggering backward.

One of her pointy heels caught the hem of her silver gown, and down she went with a yelp and a heavy thud. Her champagne flute fell to the ground and shattered.

I stepped toward Kheppy, raising a hand. "I don't know what you've got planned, sweetheart, but I can take this from here. Isn't that right, Eleanor?"

Eleanor's panicked gaze bounced between me and the tiger. "This thing belongs to you?"

I frowned. "Khepeset is hardly a thing, Eleanor. She deserves more respect than that. And she certainly doesn't belong to me. She doesn't belong to anyone. Do you, Khep?"

The great cat glared at Eleanor, muscles rippling beneath her striped coat as she gave a slow, deliberate shake of her head.

Eleanor whimpered. "Don't let her get near me. Whatever you want, you can have it. Just keep it away from me."

I considered her offer. "You know, there is something I want. I want the truth. I want to know what happened at the Channel Hotel all those years ago."

She froze, first in fear, then shock. As she sat on the flagstones, her aggression seemed to drain from her. "I had to do it," she said. "I had to protect my father. I had to protect our family name."

It wasn't the confession I'd been expecting. It raised more questions than it answered, but she was only talking because she thought I'd already worked it out. I had to keep up the ruse to keep her talking. "That must have been difficult."

I winced. Would she see through my deceit? Would she realize I didn't know as much as she thought?

Luckily for me, Eleanor seemed too wrapped up in her own misery to notice I was winging it.

"Maureen Calvert didn't want that place," she said, staring at her hands as she opened and closed her fists, as if she could still feel the aftershock of the energy she'd unleashed. "She already had plans to sell, and for peanuts, my father said. When he made an offer, she raised the price. She knew he had money. Nothing but a two-bit gold digger. Then she dangled herself in front of him like bait, hoping he would sweeten his deal. He fell for it, even when I told him he was a fool. He said I was too young, that I couldn't understand. Men can be so stupid."

She practically spat those last words. Anger laced her voice, but sadness too.

"You're right about that," I said, mostly to keep her talking.

Eleanor glanced up, surprised or relieved that I was agreeing with her.

"I was right, especially about her. He wouldn't listen. That's when I knew I had to take care of it myself. That I could show him how wrong he was. I thought she'd leave town if the place burned down. I never meant to kill her or anybody else."

My stomach knotted. My gaze darted around, looking for someone—*anyone*—to witness her confession. Seeing no one but Kheppy, I thought of what Merle had told me about making voice notes on his phone. I worked my hand into my pocket, found my device, and when she glanced away, I tapped the recording button.

"You're saying you started the Channel Hotel fire?" I asked, hoping she'd repeat the confession.

Eleanor nodded, her mascara smudged in messy streaks across her cheeks. "I just wanted her to leave and to leave my father alone, but she got in the way. She saw me using my power to set the back porch on fire. When she came at me, I was only trying to defend myself. The force hit her, and she fell."

I glanced at Kheppy, who held her ground, gaze sharp. My own thoughts scrambled, trying to make sense of the story unraveling in front of me and hoping my phone was picking up every word.

"You were so young." I quickly tabulated the years.

"Thirteen doesn't feel young when you're angry," she said. "I thought I'd sneaked out of the house without my father's knowledge, but he pulled up soon after it all started. He saw what I'd done. He told me to get in the car and had the driver take me home."

She rubbed her brow like the memory pained her.

"What did he do?" I asked. I had to keep her talking.

"He stayed. He told me later that Maureen woke up before the firefighters arrived and that she'd run off. That's what he told everyone. All these years, I've wanted to believe it. But I always knew the truth. I knew I'd killed her."

The confession nearly knocked the wind out of me, but I still wanted to know about Fiona.

"The reporter," I said carefully. "Did she figure it out?"

Pale and trembling, Eleanor shook her head. "Daddy made sure his name disappeared—from every report, every official record. And Cornelia scrubbed it from the news stories."

Of course she had. Just as a good gatekeeper would.

"But that reporter," Eleanor went on, "found a single line in the police dispatcher's log—one mention that Charles Voss was on the scene. That was all she needed. She was going to claim he'd hidden his involvement because he'd set the fire himself to force Maureen to run or risk being blamed for it. She came to me. Told me she'd found proof he'd bought the property through a shell corporation after it was abandoned to prevent any investigations. She said it was proof he was guilty."

It was a reasonable theory, and one I'd probably believe, too, if I hadn't heard the real culprit's confession.

"Why did she even care about that old place?" Eleanor whined. "She was only sniffing around, trying to find her next scandal."

"It was more than that," I said. "Fiona was Maureen's granddaughter."

Eleanor stiffened. "What difference does that make? You should've heard the things she said about my father. She was going to print horrible lies. I had to protect him."

"So you killed her too?" I said, my mind reeling as the pieces of her story fell into place.

"What?" Eleanor's eyes went wide. "Did Tom tell you that?" A sneer slid across her face as she scoffed. "That sleazeball. I knew I couldn't trust him."

Was he in on it? Had they done it together? My mind reeled.

"He's only going to be mayor because of me. My money and influence bought him that office. You'd think he'd be grateful, but no. He's greedy. I didn't think he was smart enough to suspect I had anything to do with Fiona's death, but he surprised me. I shouldn't have missed that dinner with him and Cornelia after the town hall."

Her gaze flicked toward the dark hedges, as if she half-expected him to step out of the shadows. "At first, he just wanted reassurance that it wouldn't derail the campaign. Then he wanted cash. A lot of it."

I wondered if that was the fat envelope I'd seen them exchange on the street.

Her voice cracked into a whisper. "So I gave it to him. I had to keep him happy, so it would all stay buried. But nothing ever stays buried forever, does it?"

The final pieces of the story clicked into place with grim, undeniable clarity.

I reached out and rubbed the soft fur between Kheppy's ears, needing the warmth and comfort of her presence. The deep rumble of her tiger purr vibrated through the air, soothing me.

"So you killed Maureen Calvert to keep her away from your father, and you killed Fiona because she was going to blame that fire on your father." They were no longer questions. Just sad, regrettable facts.

"I had to do it," Eleanor snapped. "They both deserved it. They gave me no choice."

She believed that. She really believed it. Her ripped gown and smeared makeup were tragic, but it was that look of genuine bewilderment—like she was the victim—that tore at my heart.

"You could have told the truth," I said. "You could have told Fiona you started that fire."

Headlights flashed through the trees, and the sound of a car engine approached.

Eleanor's tear-filled eyes went wide. She glanced at Kheppy, and I could see her mentally calculating whether she could outrun a predator built for speed. Spoiler alert: She wouldn't make it three feet.

Before Eleanor could do anything stupid, I lunged for the nearest table, grabbed an empty champagne bottle, and smashed it against the table's edge. The sound echoed through the night as I raised the jagged glass between us.

"The tiger won't hurt you," I warned. "But I might. So you'd better stay put."

Kheppy let out a low, warning growl that rippled through the air like distant thunder.

"Khep," I whispered to her, "you should go. Someone might see you."

Her shimmering orange eyes met mine. "She has seen me."

"I can take care of her," I said, waving the broken bottle again for emphasis.

"Boo! Are you here?"

Merle's voice rang through the darkness, followed by the unmistakable sound of boots stomping through dried leaves and gravel.

"I'm here! On the patio!" I called, spinning toward the light.

When I turned to Kheppy, I caught the last swish of her silver-striped tail slipping into the hedge.

A second later, Merle came jogging up the path, flashlight in hand. Behind him, Ernie Platt with his usual detective scowl, and then my sister, Delphine.

Delphine clucked her tongue the moment she saw me. "I knew she'd be here. If there's trouble, my sister always manages to be in the middle of it."

"Nice to see you too, Del." I lowered the broken bottle. My knees finally gave out, and I sank into one of the patio chairs.

Eleanor, for her part, didn't run. Not because she had a change of heart, I was sure, but because she knew it was pointless.

"Detective," I said, nodding toward the woman still sitting on the ground. "You're going to want to talk to her."

He moved closer to Eleanor and pulled a small notebook from the pocket of his trench coat.

"I'm all ears, Ms. Voss."

She looked up at him, eyes glassy with defeat.

I let my head drop back and felt the weight of the night's events lift a little. Then a warm hand settled on my shoulder—steady, familiar.

"Are you okay?" Merle's voice was a soothing balm for my ragged nerves.

He'd changed out of the muddy clothes he'd been wearing at the Channel Hotel ruins into a clean flannel shirt, fresh jeans, and his favorite cowboy hat. His eyes—steady, blue, and painfully sincere—fixed on me like I was the only thing in the world that mattered.

"I will be," I said, and I meant it.

Because even though my whole body ached from Eleanor's magical tantrum and sheer exhaustion, the truth was finally out.

For Maureen.
For Fiona.
And for me.

Chapter 29

At Peace

THE BELL ABOVE THE Halloween Boo-tique's door greeted me with a cheerful jingle as I stepped inside and braced
for another ghost-induced mess. To my surprise, the shop
was intact. No knocked-over potions or scattered tarot
cards. Nothing overturned or in disarray at all.

"Is Fiona gone?" I asked Kheppy, who sauntered in behind me, sniffing the air and poking her nose into a display
of plush tarantulas like she half-expected one to jump out
of the bin.

"I'm not sure," Kheppy said as she circled around the
spiders. "I don't sense her presence, but she has fooled me
before."

After everything my feline friend had been through with
that woman's spirit, I couldn't blame her for being cau-
tious. The night before had clearly taken something out
of her. Even though she seemed to have mastered shifting
between forms, the effort drained her.

By the time I'd gotten home after giving my statement to
Detective Platt, I was running on fumes. He'd made me go

over the story more than once, which was understandable, but I'd worried it wouldn't hold up without mentioning Eleanor's magical meltdown or Kheppy's tiger-sized intervention. Luckily, Platt and his colleagues seemed content to believe she'd attacked me to protect her family's name and fortune, and I defended myself with the broken champagne bottle.

"Murder usually boils down to love or money," the detective had said, giving a tired shake of his floppy head of hair. Judging by the state of it, he hadn't bothered with a brush before racing to the scene.

"Or love of money," I'd replied. "She may have been trying to protect her father's reputation when she killed Fiona, but my guess is she was also protecting his fortune, which is now her fortune." I didn't say it to the detective, but I couldn't help wondering if her attack on Maureen Calvert fell into the same category.

That was for the courts to decide. My part was done. Fiona's unfinished business was finally finished, with the added bonus of clearing Maureen Calvert's innocent name.

By the time I got home and found my sweet, furry friend curled up in her usual spot on the bed, fast asleep, I was more than happy to crawl in beside her. I didn't even grumble when Delphine mentioned she'd sent Zelda home with nothing more than a warning to stay away.

Technically, we could've pressed charges—for the rock through the window, the trespassing, and the general chaos—but Del had made an excellent point. If the police questioned Zelda too closely, there was a good chance she'd start rambling about Cornelia Sloane being a vampire. My sister had let the vandal believe we were being merciful when, in truth, we were just protecting our own tails—magical and otherwise. And the fact that Kheppy's little hypnotic episode had scrambled Zelda's memory of the night didn't hurt either.

By the time sunlight slipped through the curtains a few hours later, the exhaustion had eased, but the unease hadn't. Part of me wanted to call Sissy and say the shop would stay closed another day. A bigger part couldn't wait to tell Fiona about Eleanor—and I didn't know if it would set her free from whatever tethered her to this world, but she deserved to know what had happened.

As I struck a match to light the shop's protection candle, filling the air with the familiar and comforting scent of sage, eucalyptus, and lemon, I searched for the ghost.

"Fiona? Are you here?" I said.

No blown fuses. No unsettling cold spots. Just Kheppy and me and the Boo-tique.

My little companion padded up to me, her gray tail held high. She sniffed again, then leaped onto the counter beside the candle.

"She is not here." She curled her tail around her paws.

I exhaled, long and low. "You're sure?"

Kheppy nodded.

"She must have found what she needed." The cat's tone was uncharacteristically gentle.

The front door jingled again.

"I brought tea," Delphine said, breezing in with two travel mugs in one hand and a bundle of envelopes in the other. "The tea is a new blend. Lemon balm with a touch of lavender. Very calming."

My droopy eyelids were telling me something stronger would have been a better choice, but beggars couldn't be choosers.

My sister's sharp gaze swept the room.

"No mess?" she asked.

I shook my head. "No sign of our resident ghost at all."

Del placed her things on the counter beside Kheppy, who gave them a cursory sniff. "It feels"—she closed her eyes and rolled her shoulders—"different. I want to say *lighter*." She opened her eyes and tilted her head. "Do you think she's moved on?"

"We were just discussing that." I reached for a mug and sipped the fragrant tea. "Last night might have ended it for her."

Delphine made a soft, content sound, then reached into her pocket and pulled out a small muslin bag tied with twine. "Just in case. Chamomile, lavender, and a pinch of hyssop to bring peace. Can't hurt."

I took the bundle and tucked it near the register. "Couldn't agree more. Thank you."

I made a mental note to do a full sage cleansing as soon as I had the energy.

For a few quiet moments, we sipped in silence. Then Delphine asked gently, "Are you okay?"

"Just tired. A little frayed around the edges."

She patted my arm. "You did a lot for that girl. Fiona can rest easy because of you. Now that Eleanor has been arrested, she won't be able to pressure Cornelia to keep her family name out of the news anymore. Maureen will finally be vindicated."

I nodded, throat tight. "I hope so. Thank you for being there. For all of it."

Del shrugged, fussing with the display of broom-shaped pens. "Of course. You're my sister. If you jump into a fire, I'll be right there with the aloe vera gel."

I laughed softly and lifted my cup. "That sounds about right."

A shimmer of movement caught my eye—a soft shift of light in the corner of the shop. For a second, I thought it might be Fiona. But no. No chill. No buzzing presence. Just a trick of the morning sun filtering through the glass above the door.

Still, I lit a small lavender-scented votive candle and placed it in the window. Just in case Fiona was watching. Just in case she needed a little light for her travels.

Kheppy purred from her perch, her tail twitching. "Nice touch."

I saw Merle through the door's glass a second before he pushed it open, bringing with him a strong whiff of black coffee. He wore a fresh shirt—blue and green plaid—over dark jeans, and his cowboy hat tilted just right.

He crossed his hefty arms over his chest and gave me a crooked grin. "Eleanor's goose is good and cooked," he said. "Even without your recording of her confession—if that's what it was—Platt says he has more than enough to keep her locked up for a long time."

I stiffened. "What do you mean—*if that's what it was*? You heard it, didn't you? She admitted everything."

He shrugged. "Maybe. But it was hard to make out. Next time you record a murder confession, you should point the microphone toward the speaker. All I could hear was rustling—you must've had it pressed against your palm."

My pocket, actually, but I wasn't about to mention it.

"You could still hear it, right?" I asked.

He smiled and nodded. "There was enough, and she's cooperating. She told the detective about both murders."

Sissy walked in just in time to hear those last words. "Both murders? There was another one?" Her hands flew to her throat.

"It happened a long time ago," I said. "Before you were even born."

I pressed my fingers to my forehead as the weight of that realization settled over me.

Sissy brightened. "Well, I'm just glad everyone's okay." Her brow furrowed. "You are okay, right?"

The question caught me off guard. Why did everyone keep asking me that?

Merle moved closer and touched my shoulder. "You've been through a lot these past few days. If you need some time…"

I put my hand over his and smiled. "I'm fine. Really." I figured if I kept saying it, it would have to be true.

His chin dipped as he held my gaze. "You did good, Boo."

I shrugged, suddenly self-conscious. "I stumbled through it. Mostly driven by caffeine and spite."

His smile softened. "I'm pretty sure that big heart of yours played a role."

"I'll second that," Delphine said and lifted her travel mug.

"Me too," Sissy added. "I'd toast, but I forgot my coffee at home."

Delphine's gaze bounced between me and Merle. Then she smiled. "If you don't mind tea, we can brew something for you in the back. C'mon, let's see what we can find."

As my sister ushered my shop clerk toward the back, she shot me a not-so-subtle wink.

The moment they disappeared through the curtain, Kheppy gave me a look that clearly said *good luck*, then padded after them with her usual air of feline indifference.

I stayed where I was, fingers wrapped around my mug. Merle shifted his weight, but I spoke before he could.

"Merle," I said, not quite meeting his eyes. "Can I ask you something weird?"

He grinned. "You mean weirder than usual?"

I gave a half-laugh and rolled my eyes, but the nerves in my stomach didn't budge. "Could you... would you mind asking Rupert to check on Fiona? Just to see if she's all right."

Merle's posture softened. "You want to ask Rupert for a favor?"

"I know. He wouldn't usually be my first choice, but he reached her before." I finally looked at him. "I just really need to know."

His face went still. "Boo…"

I hesitated. "And maybe I'm also trying to be less mad at him. Just a little."

That earned a smile. "I think he'd appreciate that. He's been trying, you know. Trying to make things right. Okay, give me a second."

Merle exhaled and shook his shoulders, which I guess put him into a more ghost-receptive state.

He didn't say anything right away. Just stared off into the middle distance, the way he always did when Rupert was doing something ghostly I couldn't see. A few seconds passed, then a breeze stirred the air, lifting the corner of my oversized T-shirt and fluttering the feathers of the fake ravens on a nearby shelf.

I knew that breeze.

"Rupert?" I asked.

Merle nodded. "He's here."

More silence. Merle closed his eyes for a beat, then opened them again.

"He found her," he whispered. "Fiona's spirit is at peace. She's ready to move on."

I swallowed the lump forming in my throat. "She is?"

"Yeah. But she asked me—Rupert, really—to tell you thank you. And goodbye."

The words hit hard. Not in a sad way, exactly—more like relief. Like something wrong had finally been set right.

I nodded, not trusting my voice right away. "Thank you," I whispered. I wasn't even sure if I was saying it to Merle or Rupert or Fiona. Maybe all three.

Merle touched my hand. "She's ready to go, Boo. You made that happen."

The air between us changed. Maybe saying goodbye to Fiona had opened a door I hadn't realized was shut.

Merle must've felt it too, because after a moment, he looked at me again—more intently this time.

"I was worried about you. Worried about us, really."

I froze. "Us? What do you mean?"

"I know it's been messy. I know I've made things harder sometimes. But I care about you, Boo. I hope you know that."

I stared at him, my heart thumping harder than I cared to admit. I took his hand.

"How about we start with dinner—a nice, quiet meal to celebrate—" My eyes flew wide. "Oh my gosh. The election!"

With everything that had happened, it had completely slipped my mind. Honestly, I had to be the worst campaign manager in history.

"Did you get the results yet?" I asked. "Should we be planning a celebration... or your inauguration?"

He glanced down, chuckled, and rubbed his lips. "Yes, I got the results, but, no, we don't need to plan anything."

"Wait. What?" I touched my forehead. "Tom Dodge won? How is that possible?" I mentally started organizing a recall campaign. He wasn't fit to be mayor. The man had been blackmailing Eleanor. Sure, she was a murderer, but...

That grin on Merle's face widened as he shook his head again. "It wasn't Tom. Glen won."

"You're kidding." He had to be pulling my leg.

He shrugged. "It's true. The city clerk said it wasn't even close. To be honest, I'm relieved. I don't want to be mayor, and Chef Glen will do a fine job."

"I guess there's a lesson in that," I said. "Never underestimate the power of free sliders."

"How about I pick you up when the shop closes and we head over to the Beachside Café for dinner, and to congratulate Chef Glen, of course."

"I'd like that."

He gave my hand another squeeze, then released it. "I'll let you get back to work. I'll call you later."

"You better."

As the door closed behind him, morning sunlight spilled into the shop like warm honey. Kheppy hopped onto the counter beside me and settled in with practiced grace.

"You like him," she said, tilting her head.

"Don't sound so smug."

"Then I am right."

I sighed. "Fine. You win. I do like him. I hope you do too."

She hesitated—just long enough to make me nervous. "I do."

I chuckled with relief and, for the first time in a long time, things actually felt right.

I glanced around the Boo-tique. The shelves were full. A candle flickered gently behind the register. Everything, for once, seemed to be at peace.

Outside, a young couple stopped to admire Petunia, my witchy mannequin holding court in the front window. A little girl pressed her nose to the glass, giggling at the animatronic raven with glowing red eyes staring back at her.

I stepped behind the counter, drew in a deep breath, and let it out slowly.

The shop might not be haunted anymore—but it was still mine. And it was home.

As I pushed the stack of envelopes to a safer distance away from the candle, I noticed the one I'd been avoiding. The pale cream envelope with my name written in looping, elegant handwriting lay on the top. Its New Orleans postmark stared at me.

My chest tightened. I'd been putting off opening this one, telling myself I'd deal with it when life stopped spinning. Maybe that time had finally come.

I tore the seal and unfolded the single sheet inside. Lila's handwriting—rounded, confident, and achingly familiar—filled the page. She wrote about the French Quarter, a new job, and how she'd been thinking of me lately. Then, near the bottom, one simple line caught my breath:

I'm planning a visit soon, Mom. I hope that's okay.

A spark of joy fluttered in my chest—quick and bright—but it was chased by a pulse of nerves. We hadn't seen each other in years.

And yet... there was something else. The letter tried so hard to sound cheerful, but beneath the tidy handwriting, I could feel it: something unsaid, something uneasy.

Kheppy brushed against my arm, her fur charged with a faint static hum. "Good news?" she asked softly.

"I think so," I said, folding the letter with care. "But I can't shake the feeling there's more to it."

The cat's tawny eyes narrowed. "The air feels... strange," she murmured. "Something stirs."

A flicker of movement caught my eye. The shop candle trembled, its flame bending and flaring as though answering some distant call. Shadows rippled along the walls, then settled again.

Kheppy's ears twitched. "She is coming."

I swallowed hard, unsure whether she meant Lila or something else entirely.

The candle steadied, its flame now burning a shade brighter.

"Looks like peace and quiet didn't last long," I murmured.

Kheppy's whiskers quivered, and she gave a knowing look. "It never does."

Ready to follow the clues alongside Boo and Kheppy in Moonlight, Magic, and Murder, the next book in the Laguna Bay Midlife Witch Cozy Mystery series? Grab it at https://DeAnnaDrake.com/LagunaBay3.

Free Novella (Subscriber Exclusive)

GRAB *DEAD END DATE*, a free novella available exclusively to members of my Cozy Mystery Readers Club. The book is part of the Purr-fect Relic series, which is where Boo and Khepeset first made their debut. Within its pages you'll discover how Rebecca and Khepeset's sister, Aneksi, hunt down a killer during Rebecca's first date with Detective Nick Devon at Citrus Grove's hottest new nightspot. *Dead End Date* can be read as a stand-alone story, but it fits chronologically between *Paws, Claws, and Curses* and *Hisses, Hexes, and Homicide*.

When you join me and other cozy mystery readers in the Cozy Mystery Readers Club, you'll also have access to free puzzles, book-related recipes, behind-the-scenes tidbits, and other bonus content. Sign up at DeAnnaDrake. com/join. It's free and easy, and you won't miss any of the fun!

Dear Reader

THANK YOU FOR TAKING the time to read *Ghosts, Lies, and Alibis*, the second book in the Laguna Bay Midlife Witch Cozy Mystery series. It's such a joy to share the adventures — and misadventures — of these Laguna Bay characters, who have completely captured my heart and added so much to the magical cats universe, which includes the Citrus Grove gang in the Purr-fect Relic Cozy Mysteries.

If these characters have earned a soft spot in your book-loving heart, it would mean so much to me if you could jot a few words in a review at your favorite retailer. Good reviews and positive word of mouth are extremely helpful to an author and always deeply appreciated.

Bonus Recipe: Zelda's Chewy Red Velvet Cake Cookies

ZELDA'S CHEWY RED VELVET CAKE COOKIES

Yield: About 24 cupcakes | Prep Time: 10 minutes | Bake Time: 9–11 minutes

—ℓℓ—

Ingredients:

- 1 box red velvet cake mix (15.25 oz)
- 1/3 cup vegetable oil
- 2 large eggs
- 1 tsp pure vanilla extract
- 2 tbsp cocoa powder (for extra chocolate depth)
- 1/2 cup semisweet chocolate chips

- 1/2 cup white chocolate chips (optional, but Zelda insists because it "makes them prettier")
- Powdered sugar, for rolling

Instructions:

Preheat the oven to 350°F (175°C). Line two baking sheets with parchment paper.

Mix the cake mix, cocoa powder, oil, eggs, and vanilla in a large bowl until well combined. The dough will be thick and glossy. Fold in the chocolate chips.

Scoop tablespoon-sized balls and roll them lightly in powdered sugar. Place them 2 inches apart on the baking sheet. Bake 9–11 minutes, just until the edges are set and the tops are slightly crinkled. Cool on the pan for 2 minutes, then transfer to a rack.

Zelda's Tips:

- For extra decadence, press a few chocolate chips on top right after baking.
- Sprinkle a pinch of cinnamon or cayenne in the batter for a little bite.

A Recipe Note from Zelda:

If you've ever been accused of being too much, these cookies are for you. Too red, too rich, too chocolatey—and far too good to share with anyone who doesn't appreciate a little drama along with their dessert.

I first baked these Chewy Red Velvet Cake Cookies for the Laguna Bay Women's Club—mostly to outshine my neighbor's lemon bars (and I did, thank you very much). The secret is to underbake them slightly and let them cool on the pan. That's when the magic happens—the chewy centers, the crackly edges, and that deep, dark cocoa kiss.

Just don't leave the plate unattended. Someone's liable to sneak one... or three.

Books by DeAnna Drake and the Author's Other Work

LAGUNA BAY MIDLIFE WITCH COZY MYSTERY SERIES

Candy, Cauldrons, and a Corpse
Ghosts, Lies, and Alibis
Moonlight, Magic, and Murder

MAGICAL CATS COZY MYSTERY SERIES

Trouble at the Christmas Tea (novella)
Lady Paws and the Christmas Caper (short story)

A PURR-FECT RELIC COZY MYSTERY SERIES

Paws, Claws, and Curses
Dead End Date (novella)
Hisses, Hexes, and Homicide
Furballs and Felonies

Crime and Cat-astrophes
Blackmail and Kitty Tails
Whiskers and Ciphers

A MAGICAL MOUSE CAPER SERIES

Mouse in the House

—ell—

FANTASY FICTION
WRITTEN AS D.D. CROIX

THE QUEEN'S FAYTE SERIES

Memory Thief (prequel story)
Dragonfly Maid
Slivering Curse
Shadow Rite
Guardian of the Realm

ere

HISTORICAL AND CONTEMPORARY ROMANCE WRITTEN AS DEANNA CAMERON

THE DANCER CHRONICLES

The Girl on the Midway Stage
The Girl on the Vaudeville Stage

CALIFORNIA BELLY DANCE ROMANCE SERIES

Shimmy for Me
Dance with Me
Jingly Bells

About DeAnna Drake

DeAnna Drake writes warm, witty, magical cozy mysteries filled with heart, humor, and unforgettable feline companions.

Her books blend the charm of small-town cozies with the depth of character-driven fantasy—where ancient magic lingers, secrets refuse to stay buried, and talking cats with centuries of history always seem to know more than they're saying.

DeAnna is the author of the *Purr-fect Relic Cozy Mystery* series and the *Laguna Bay Midlife Witch Cozy Mysteries*, two interconnected worlds tied together by long-lived magical cats, cursed relics, supernatural politics, and found-family bonds. Readers love her stories for their emotional resonance, rich world-building, relatable midlife heroines, and the blend of mystery, magic, and heart.

If you enjoy cozy escapes with layered characters, gentle humor, twisty mysteries, and a touch of ancient wonder, you'll feel right at home in the Magical Cats Universe.

Under different names, DeAnna writes young-adult fantasy fiction, contemporary romances, and historical novels set in the Victorian and Edwardian eras.

When she isn't plotting new adventures for her characters, she enjoys afternoon tea, binging crime shows, and escaping to Disneyland whenever she can.

She lives in Southern California with her family, which includes her two favorite people and one ridiculously pampered border collie. Learn more at https://DeAnna Drake.com.

Facebook:
https://www.facebook.com/DeAnnaDrakeWrites
Instagram:
https://www.instagram.com/DeAnnaDrakeAuthor